遥有一星似我源

莲芳的诗与画

高莲芳 著

Yonder Star

Lilian's Poems and Paintings

复旦大学出版社

序

儿时，诵读"鹅，鹅，鹅，曲项向天歌"；
少年时，"飞流直下三千尺，疑似银河落九天"；
青年时，"曾经沧海难为水，除却巫山不是云"；
求学时，"我怎么能把你来比作夏天，你不独比它可爱也比它温婉？"
闲暇时，我喜欢读艾米莉·狄金森：

一个萼片，一叶花瓣，和一根荆棘
在一个普通的夏日晨曦——
一瓶露水——一只或两只蜜蜂——
一缕轻风——一株马槟榔长在树林里——
而我，则是一朵玫瑰！

我的心跟着诗歌律动。诗歌之美，犹如蓝天里飘浮的自由云朵，又如大海上泛起的粼粼波光，也如阳台上绽放的粉色牡丹，给我的生活带来了希望与激情。每当我提起笔来涂鸦写点诗的时候，总能感觉到我又回到了内心的小女孩最纯粹的灵魂，想去探索未知的世界，满怀好奇，充满了期待。她的心在怦然跳动，红扑扑的脸颊折射阳光的灿烂。

当我随着内心的感动写下这一首首诗歌的时候，觉得也许没有人会有机会读到它，它将被封存在我的书堆和文件夹中，慢慢销声匿迹，渐渐被遗忘。但是，每当学生和我聊天、谈起生活和理想的时候，总会不自觉地提及诗和远方。诚然，无论时代如何变化，人对美的追求始终如一，对诗意的向往始终如一。

衷心感谢杨辉教授和曹珍芬女士为我打开了一道门，也感谢您，我亲爱的读者，欣然走进这道门。您现在手捧着的《遥有一星似我源——莲芳的诗与画》，是一位十分平凡的英语教师心中的诗和远方。当您翻阅的时候，我倍感荣幸，能够与您分享语言之美与生活之味。诗的插图也都是我亲手为您绘制的，希望您在这方寸之间尽情享受您心中的诗和远方。

谨以此书献上我最美好的祝福。

高莲芳

2021年5月28日

目录

Part I   Nature 自然感悟 / 1

1 A Tree 一棵树 /2

2 The Idyllic Xanadu 世外桃源 /4

3 Stars 繁星 /6

4 Typhoon and Rainbow 台风与彩虹 /8

5 Photographers 摄影师 /10

6 Sadness 悲伤 /12

7 I Imagine 幻想 /14

8 I Never 未竟之旅 /16

9 Hypnosis 好眠 /18

10 Butterfly's Despair 落蝶 /20

11 The Spring 春 /22

12 A Scene of Rich Spring 富春图 /24

13 The Mourning Season 清明时节 /26

14 A Peony Garden 牡丹园 /28

15 The Morning Glory 牵牛花 /30

16 Nature's Greetings 自然的问候 /32

17 A Seed 种子 /34

18 Golden Autumn 金秋 /36

19 Gingko 银杏 /38

20 Instinct 天性 /40

21 Big Cats About the House "巨猫"绕屋 /42

22 Gardening 空中花园 /44

23 I Stand Where Peach Blossoms Bloom 在那桃花盛开的地方 /46

24 Sowing Seeds 播种 /48

25 Golden Fish Among Lotus Leaves 莲间金鱼 /50

26 My Acrobatic Fish 吾养巧技金鳞 /52

27 Golden Lake and Golden Mean 金湖之旅与中庸之道 /54

28 Sun Flowers 向日葵 /56

29 Autumn 秋 /58

30 Night 夜 /60

31 Sky: My Primer Book 儿时看"天"书 /62

32 Nature 自然 /64

Part II　Life 生活点滴 / 67

1 A Debt to Life 生活之恩 /68

2 Love Is Free 爱本无价 /70

3　Country Dwellers and City Dwellers　城里郊外 /72

4　An Elegant Lady　所谓伊人 /74

5　Ode to Fruits　水果颂 /76

6　Sealed with Three Kisses　三吻之诺 /78

7　Sharing　共享 /80

8　Tranquility　那刻宁静 /82

9　Is It Too Old to Bear A Child?　孩子，你来晚了吗？ /84

10　Stories　佳话人间 /86

11　Lost Things and Friends　失物与故人 /88

12　Library　图书馆 /90

13　Playing Basketball　打篮球 /92

14　The London Conflagration　伦敦烈火 /94

15　Connection　心有所系 /96

16　Melancholy　心愁 /98

17　Save Our Children　救救孩童 /100

18　Food Got Burnt　污馐记 /102

19　The Tune in Thee　心头的旋律 /104

20　Recalling All the Good Times in No. 3 Girls' Middle School　忆市三女中 /106

21　A Miraculous Reunion　重逢 /108

22　Love, Pity and Mercy　爱、怜与慈悲 /110

23　Too Poor to Look Down Upon Money-Making　关于金钱 /112

24　One Girl's Doll Is Another's Devil　招娣 /114

25 The Death of a Centenarian 期颐离世 /116

26 The International Yoga Day 国际瑜伽日 /118

27 On Diet 节食 /120

28 On Children's Day 儿童节 /122

29 On Free Chinese Ink and Wash Painting 大写意中国水墨画 /124

30 Love Box 爱之盒 /126

31 The Declination 拒绝 /128

32 The Power of Literature 文学之力 /130

33 Isabella 伊莎贝拉 /132

34 Mannerly Neighborhood 贤邻 /134

35 In Guilin 桂林游 /136

36 A Surgery 记手术 /138

37 Metropolitan Loneliness 寂寞都市 /140

38 The Story of Pomegranates 石榴记 /142

39 Happy Teachers' Day 咏师 /144

40 The Secrets of Long Life 长寿的秘诀 /146

41 A Good Husband Is Hard to Find 佳偶难寻 /148

42 A Confession 自白 /150

43 For Procrastinators 致拖延症 /152

44 In Father's Name 以父之名 /154

45 The Meaning of Posterity 后浪 /156

46 Thanksgiving 感恩 /158

47 Ode to Poetry Lovers 诗歌爱好者颂 /160

48　Never Say Goodbye to BNU　再会，北师大 /162

49　5∶30　卯时二刻 /164

50　Fathers Are More Welcomed　爸爸更受欢迎 /166

51　No Empty Seats in Starbucks　星巴克满座的一天 /168

52　Life's Intervals　浮生若梦眠无暇 /170

53　The 70th National Day　庆新中国70周年华诞 /172

54　A Special Gift　特殊的礼物 /174

55　The Story of the Dark Lady and Her Mum　黑美人 /176

56　New Year's Resolution　新年愿望 /178

57　My Heart's Ease　我本平静的心湖 /180

58　The Plight of an Epidemic　战"疫" /182

59　A Dream　梦境 /184

60　The Virtues of Being Quarantined　隔离之趣 /186

61　Young and Promising　年少轻狂 /188

62　A Butterfly's Dream　蝶之梦 /190

63　A Lovely Child　孩子来自天堂 /192

64　Simba and Tutu　辛巴和图图 /194

65　Backache　背疼 /196

66　Stage Fright　怯场 /197

67　A Portrait of Pomegranate　石榴图 /198

68　The Law　律法 /200

69　Human Selfishness　人类的自私 /202

70　Will Love Fade Like a Flower?　爱情是否如花凋谢？ /204

71 A Friend in Need Is a Friend Indeed 患难见真情 /206

72 A Panacea to Life's Vicissitudes 遣怀良药 /208

73 On Tenacity 坚忍不拔 /210

74 On Lending Money 记借贷 /212

75 Peace and Joy 平安喜乐 /214

76 Friends and Foes 朋友与仇敌 /216

77 Happiness, Success and Health 人生三宝 /218

78 A Remedy for Self-Restoration 自愈良方 /220

79 The Road Less Travelled: Devoted to Emily 特立独行：献给艾米莉 /222

80 Self-Reflection 吾日三省吾身 /224

81 Love 爱 /226

82 Unfamiliar Characters 生僻字 /228

83 The Heart 心灵 /230

84 I Know That I Know Nothing 自知无所知 /232

85 Nature and Life's Riddle 自然与生活之谜 /234

86 Change, Energy of Adventure 探赜索隐而求变 /236

87 Heavenly Father and Mother 天上父母 /238

88 My Friends Are My Estate 义结金兰 /240

89 When We Lose 失落有时 /242

90 Peace Is Paradise 福泰安康 /244

91 Nostalgic 怀旧 /246

92 The Cheerful Poet Society 欢乐诗社 /248

Part III　Meditation 人生思考 / 251

1　A Day's Experiment　屡试屡验 /252

2　My Clock　晨钟暮鼓 /254

3　A Year　年复一年 /256

4　Friendship in a Storm　风雨中的友情 /258

5　Reading　阅读 /260

6　The Feeblest and the Waywardest　羸弱与刚愎 /262

7　When Faith Is Lost　金石不坚 /264

8　The Simple Days　寻常的日子 /266

9　A Word　言辞 /268

10　Deviation　离经叛道 /270

11　Commitment　承诺 /272

12　Pride　傲骨 /274

13　Family　家庭 /276

14　Grit　坚毅 /278

15　Virtue, Our Walking Staff　美德是我们行路的杖 /280

16　Time and Words　时间与话语 /282

17　Health and Happiness　健康与快乐 /284

18　The Examination Day　考试日 /286

19　Passiveness　被动 /288

20　Constant Dripping Wears Through a Stone　水滴石穿 /290

21　The Slow Sparrow Needs to Start Early　笨鸟先飞 /292

Part IV Idioms 成语典故 / 295

1 A Golden Millet Dream 黄梁一梦 /296

2 The Poor Man's Backbone 廉者不受嗟来之食 /298

3 Seeing Is Believing 百闻不如一见 /300

4 Bamboos in the Mind 胸有成竹 /302

5 Thrice Calling at Zhuge Liang's Residence 三顾茅庐 /304

6 A Swan Feather from a Friend Afar 千里送鹅毛 /306

7 The Lost Steed 塞翁失马 /308

8 A Race Between the Rabbit and the Tortoise 龟兔赛跑 /310

9 To Read Upon Snow Light 映雪读书 /312

10 An Eagle and a Sparrow 雄鹰与燕雀 /314

11 Ambulation Is Transportation 安步当车 /316

12 All to One 百川归海 /318

13 A Dream of Nan Ke 南柯一梦 /320

14 To Look at a Leopard Through a Bamboo Tube 管中窥豹 /322

15 Grandsire Yu Surmounts the Mountains 愚公移山 /324

16 A Symbol of Dogged Determination 精卫填海 /326

17 To Learn from Our Companions 见贤思齐 /328

18 To Make a Sewing Needle Out of an Iron Bar 磨杵成针 /330

19 Old Horses Know the Way Home 老马识途 /332

20 To Quench Thirst by Thinking of Plums 望梅止渴 /334

21 The Reunion After Rupture 破镜重圆 /336

22 Rejuvenation 返老还童 /338

23 No Need to Worry 杞人忧天 /340

24 No Intact Eggs Within an Overturned Nest 覆巢之下安有完卵 /342

25 Skyey Mountains and Running Water 高山流水 /344

26 Bosom Friend 管鲍之交 /346

27 Death Heavier Than Mount Tai 重于泰山 /348

28 The Emperor's New Clothes 皇帝的新装 /350

29 Catching and Releasing 七擒七纵 /352

30 Talent Tested by Composing a Seven-Pace Poem 七步之才 /354

31 Complicated and Confusing 扑朔迷离 /356

32 Three Pages Without Mentioning "Donkey" 三纸无驴 /358

33 To Mistake the Shadow of Bow as Snake in the Cup 杯弓蛇影 /360

34 Mantis, Cicada and Siskin 螳螂捕蝉黄雀在后 /362

35 In the Same Boat 同舟共济 /364

跋 / 367

Part I

Nature 自然感悟

1 A Tree

I wish I were a tree planted by the river,

So I shall not live in want.

My fingers stretch high to touch the firmament

And I may give shelter for birds and farmers.

I shall drink the dew in the morn

And say adieu to the sun at dusk,

Guiding the way for whom shall ask

And bear the fruit in due season.

The cedar, the fir, the pine,

I shall be one of thine,

Tall and straight to look at afar.

My leaves are evergreen and alar.

My years are long and children multitude.

Happy is my life till infinitude.

一棵树

我愿变作一棵树栽在溪水边,
因此我便不至于匮乏。
我的指尖可触及穹苍,
为鸟儿农夫遮挡风雨。

我可以朝饮甘露,
在黄昏言别落日,
为求索的人指路,
按时候结出果实。

松树杉树香柏树,
我是你们中之一,
高大挺拔望向远处,
树叶有翼四季常青。

年岁久远子孙无数,
日子快活直到永远。

2 The Idyllic Xanadu

Cost what it may,
I determine to seek for the ancient Xanadu.
Like the ancient boatman in May,
I prefer to take a boat perdue.

To drift along the stream,
To discover the peach blossom,
And to trace the cradle
Toward the cave crab-sidle,

To see fertile vast land with exuberant crops,
Rows of houses spick-and-span,
Mulberry trees and bamboo groves surround chimney tops.
Cocks crow and dogs bark on the crossing lane.

Hospitable folks invite me to their dwelling.
Oh, my idyllic Xanadu calling!

世外桃源

万贯尽竭我不惜,
决心笃寻桃源迹。
古人五月摇舟楫,
我亦乘舟行砥砺。

顺流而下缘溪行,
欲寻锦簇桃花林。
百花溯源寻芳境,
只随侧行螯蟹影。

良田美池入眼帘,
鳞次栉比屋舍檐。
桑荫竹影绕炊烟,
鸡鸣犬吠阡陌间。

好客村人酒食延,
恬静桃源心所恋!

3 Stars

I adore the stars in the yonder far,
Twinkling like glowworms on a velvet vault.
How old are you and how are you there?
I wondered whether it was a setting default.

On a fine and beautiful night, I went out to count
The numerous stars chatting and playing in the space.
How free and happy they were above the seamount
To taunt that simpleton for her bold ignorance?

From the very beginning they were there,
Longer than that can be fair.
God made two great lights in the aerosphere
And also multitudinous stars in the air.

I enjoyed a mysterious original relation with the universe,
As if I belong to one of the stars high above there.

繁星

远际繁星慕于衷,
熠熠流萤舞鹅绒。
几欢几愁几春冬,
疑是盘古定横纵。

良夜信步数星斗,
繁星窃语相嬉逗。
跃然海崖逍遥游,
嘲笑人间昧蜉蝣。

太初已然置于天,
难言公平论久远。
日升月明阴晴圆,
众星不计缀苍颜。

神秘寰宇心有缘,
遥有一星似我源。

4 Typhoon and Rainbow

Nepartak is approaching and everyone is on alert.
When we pop
At the mountain foot,
Fine and serene, mist and clouds surround the top.

With the eye of the heaven
Scorching in the sky,
A dark cloud comes
With drizzles and drops.

A rainbow, like an arch
Appears and floats
In the middle of the sea of clouds,
Rendering everyone hope and cheers.

"Red, orange, yellow, green, blue, violet and indigo,"
My son proclaims, "Life is colorful!"

台风与彩虹

将临台风尼伯特,
我等疾步心忐忑。
行至山脚天晴澈,
云雾缭绕将顶遮。

恰逢天眼正执事,
金刚怒目当空视。
滚滚黑云奔腾至,
淅淅沥沥洒天匙。

一弓彩虹弯如镰,
缥缈浮光入眼帘。
苍茫云海其中现,
欢欣鼓舞喜笑颜。

赤橙黄绿青蓝紫,
儿曰生活多彩姿。

5 Photographers

The "photographers" take photos,
But I photo them.
The scenery is not the scenery
But they that appear in my poem.

Everyone is a photographer today,
Qualified or lousy
With great confidence and passion,
Posting their pictures online for sharing.

For showing off or recording events,
Both with a purpose
Of meaning creation,
Or for recollection.

Historians retell past stories,
While photographers draw life alive pictures.

摄影师

摄影师摄影,
不知入我景。
我景非我镜,
其境诗中映。

摄影者不稀,
良莠各不齐。
斗志昂扬意,
晒图求相递。

记事或自矜,
两者皆有心。
或为一创新,
或留往事印。

史家述远近,
影师绘生灵。

6 Sadness

A deep sadness crawled over my mind,
Without any reason it seems.
Maybe there were too many reasons
Or it was just a touch of sadness?

Past things replay like a movie,
Triggering my failure, disappointment and disillusions.
I cannot combat
A battle so great.

The heart's best companion should not be sadness,
Because it adds burden and weight
To her lovingkindness and goodness,
While joy is just right.

May it be just a dream,
I am awakened by a beam.

悲伤

一缕悲思上心头,
其似莫名无缘由。
或其有因千万绺,
或其徒然平添愁?

幕幕往事如影现,
颓靡失意空黯然。
无力能消心麻乱,
焦灼愁烦莫能战。

忧愁不应心相伴,
徒增苦累添负担,
仁慈暖爱心本善,
笑逐颜开最当然。

愿其只为一枕梦,
光曜一道解昏蒙。

7 I Imagine

I imagine, I could fly
And abide in absolute,
And many a salute.
But what of that?

I imagine, we could live forever,
The best vitality
That excels decadence.
But what of that?

I imagine that in paradise
Somehow there will be no merchandise,
Some new society be instituted.
But what of that?

Has love found a purpose in everyone's heart
Like new-born babies with a brand new start?

幻想

浮想翩翩展翅翔,
居于永恒跨沧桑。
世人皆尊我为长,
诚然若此又如何?

浮想连连皆永生,
力壮体强龙虎腾。
万寿无疆不朽身,
诚然若此又如何?

浮想绵绵极乐界,
投机倒把皆不屑。
焕然新世相更迭,
诚然若此又如何?

岂问心中存大爱,
如新生儿思无邪?

8 I Never

I never saw a mirage;
I never saw an ocean.
Yet know I how a grain of sand looks,
And what a spray must be like.

I never spoke with a saint,
Nor visited a heavenly temple.
Yet certain am I of the paradise,
As if the atlas were given.

Nature I revere with awe.
God I love with my heart.
Noble I strive to make myself.
Demos are my folks and root.

The universe has sent an invitation to me
To explore and I feel like in a big time.

未竟之旅

未见过海市蜃楼，
未见过汪洋大海，
却识得沙砾颗颗，
却识得浪花皑皑。

圣贤哲人未谋面，
天坛圣殿未踏足，
确信天堂必设宴，
遥途路径已觉悟。

自然造化吾敬畏，
爱神爱人吾心尊，
竭力为人至尊贵，
模范为邻善为根。

琼宇设宴邀我往，
探索乾坤向天航。

9 Hypnosis

When the queen of the night ascends to the sky,
Our ancestors worshipped her with great awe and respect,
Appreciating her beauty and majesty, and I
Was encouraged to read their poetry eulogizing the crescent.

When the melancholy moon gives light unto human beings,
They relax and relieve their pains and burdens to heaven
To an oblivion and start to weave a dream of blessings.
How wonderful it is that we sleep and repose in our haven!

Yet a monster came and stole our untroubled peace and concord.
We lost our time and mind of tranquility and quietness.
It is harder for us to go to sleep naturally awaiting a promised land.
The sleepless nights call for a deep and sound hypnosis.

O, my Diana, my goddess, grant me your majestic power
Of beauty and faculty to deal with tomorrow and dolor!

好眠

静夜女王临天宫,
始祖先宗恭且崇。
服其盛威醉其美,
咏月作诗与我共。

皓月清芒泻人间,
苦恼悄逝身且翩。
酣夜酣人织酣梦,
怡神养性屋舍恬。

黠兽夜潜盗逸安,
时过神乱失静闲。
梦中乐土莫能抵,
不寐之人盼好眠。

喔,戴安娜,我的女神,请赐我
　神圣之力,
以倾国倾城之美与满腹经纶之才
　迎接明日与悲戚!

10 Butterfly's Despair

I saw you fluttering in the air,
And suddenly fall into despair,
Yellowish and light as a leaf,
Too soon to be summoned to leave.

We are all driven to Styx,
However unwilling and helpless.
Fortune's hand is made of iron.
Who says you may fix?

落蝶

我见你振翅空中，
弹指间双翼坠落，
一叶残黄任风斩，
奈何断魂听其唤。

浩瀚烟波轻如蝶，
涛卷浪覆入冥河，
天之铁网命难逃，
凡人似蝶谁能渡？

花如圆玉
莹无疵
庚子秋月
莲芳画

11 The Spring

Primroses, the love of the spring
Violets, the earliest blossom in spring
Bloom abundantly and merrily in the park,
But few were once saved in the ancient ark.

Pansies and cuckoo flowers decorate the flower-bed.
Their loud color shows off nature beauty's pride.
Bees are busy gathering nectar among the blossom,
While little birds twitter over the branches blithesome.

Daisies and daffodils leave no fruit behind.
Squirrels and sparrows start new pastime.
The swallow comes to build a new nest under our roof, an old friend.
Close friends come and sit for tea and chat anytime.

Under the spring sunshine everything starts anew.
I refresh myself and my books from the library renew.

春

迎春最能得春宠,
草紫罗兰立先功。
百花争艳园囿中,
曾上方舟寥几丛。

色堇杜鹃饰花床,
靓色多姿美自彰。
蕊间蜂簇采蜜忙,
枝上燕雀啁啾畅。

雏菊水仙无果实,
松鼠麻雀遣消时。
筑巢旧燕檐下识,
品茶叙旧友情挚。

春日旭辉万事新,
重整书斋心更清。

12 A Scene of Rich Spring

How can a wall confine all this gardenful of spring?

I put on my new self to take a new road, trying.

The reddish blossoms and the greenish willows do not belong to me.

Nature makes them to shed on us the dew of grace and glee.

富春图

满园春色关不住，
抖擞新我辟新途，
花红柳绿非我属，
造物使然尽福禄。

13 The Mourning Season

Early spring and early April becomes special
For all Chinese people,
As we mourn our deceased dearest;
As it drizzles from heaven remotest.

Some young men passed away too young and too tender.
They may not have tasted the joy and happiness of life.
Their leaving makes me sadder than the elder.
Their grey hair parents live and miss them with grief.

If in heaven they live and see,
I hope they send a message
To their friends alive to cheer —
Our place is better and a passage

From harsh reality to eternity,
Transcending human sensibility and sanity.

清明时节

仲春孟夏每相逢,
九州大地裛香尘。
星火青柱祭往者,
碧落烟雨化清痕。

犹怜殒命尚英年,
世间一遭喜难全。
逝者已逝俱往矣,
白发悲恸了余年。

在天频视若有灵,
但寄彩笺诉近情。
展信舒眉如晤面,
安好勿念相常惦。

黄泉冰冷世事艰,阴阳自古两相牵。
圣贤难解人缱绻,莫笑真情系九天。

14 A Peony Garden

A peony garden is different and distinct from ordinary gardens,
Because peony blossoms are more inviting and exuberant.
A single peony appears noble and single-minded ever since
When tossed by a breeze its baby face smiles with a jocund spirit.

A peony's apparel is incomparable,
Be it pink, white or purple,
Its flower larger and with more pedals,
Its size approximately ten times more than a daffodil.

Whichever one of the peonies you gaze at,
It will always make you complacent,
And wonder how the maker may create
Such a beautiful flower named as peony!

Gathering together in a peony garden
Is when you forget all your worldly burden,
And wish you were one of them.
Let there be no better place such as a heaven!

牡丹园

别具一格牡丹园,
繁花妖娆甚烂漫。
华丽一株意且专,
天真笑颜迎风欢。

牡丹装颜莫能比,
魏紫粉白总相宜。
花开硕硕生多蒂,
雅蒜十支仍不及。

信手随指相凝视,
百指百视乐百次。
心问造化何如此,
裁出牡丹美如斯。

牡丹园中来相聚,
尘世烦扰皆能去。
愿化一花心相许,
胜似天堂无忧虑。

15 The Morning Glory

On my balcony I sowed some flower seeds in a porcelain pot,
And waited patiently for the tender shoots to break through the soil.
Three days passed, some tender white shoots crept out of the lot,
Crowned with a bean each as if it was a canopy to protect them from broil.

The shoot kept growing from two leaves to many;
The stems and vines desired to twine and twist.
I hung some strings from the windowsill of the balcony,
Then they perceived my attending and twine happily as if advised.

Then I went on a holiday and was away from home.
I wondered one day when they were going to blossom.
The day I arrived home four of them bloomed like trumpets from heaven.
I gazed and gazed at the purplish and pinkish "trumpets" all of a sudden.

They are entitled an awesomely wonderful name of "morning glory",
Deserving so much recommendation and glorification even for one day's glory.

牵牛花

阳台陶盆播花种,
静候嫩芽破土笼。
但只三日有静动。
芽顶一篷遮日睨。

芽生新叶复生芽,
挂藤曲茎绕藤挂。
手系几绳悬窗下,
顿会我意缘之爬。

离家几日出游乐,
吐艳之日莫能测。
归时喜见紫粉色,
四株号角响天彻。

盛名又曰"晨之曜",
朝颜一现亦可褒。

16 Nature's Greetings

In the human society if you love,
Get prepared for the anguish of loss.
Your beloved one may hurt you with a countermove
With which you feel that your world collapses in a toss.

Nature's greetings will embrace you tenderly.
The morning glory blooms quietly and gently.
Returning to nature mother's bosom is the best choice.
She holds you dear without making a noise.

Morning glories are such a common flower.
They blossom towards the sun earnestly
With shapes like a trumpet blowing towards a tower,
Summoning hosts of the air to struggle fearlessly.

Greet nature and she will greet you with more wonder.
Life is short while nature endures for ever.

自然的问候

托付凡心须慎言,
痛失所爱夜难眠。
情深似海袖中箭,
地崩山摧俱灰念。

温厚离愁投大千,
牵牛淑静盛似仙。
自然怀抱胜归倦,
润物无声心自虔。

牵牛花开寻常见,
拳拳向日尽开颜。
状若海笛楼与宣,
乐冲九天扬帆劝。

投之以滴报涌泉,
薄命不比山海延。

17 A Seed

A seed there has ever been,
Lying on the country green,
Being happy in her happiness,
Waiting under shadows numberless.

She's going down under the earth
Till tender shoots burst with mirth
To see the sun shine again.
This will be the sower's gain.

Life starts with a seed.
Babies need to breed.
Family is our happy lot
In some dramatic plot.

A seed grows to be an oak tree.
A child desires to be free.

种子

绿野毓灵韵,
细种卧地藏。
无忧孕乐土,
翘首暗乌光。

根生向背天,
芽吐骤开颜。
金乌重拂面,
耕者享其年。

襁褓纳细种,
灌溉似春风。
阖家得所幸,
笑骂戏人生。

细种成巨橡,
婴儿望自由。

18 Golden Autumn

Autumn must be artistic than Picasso.
Even Monet might be overshadowed.
She dyes leaves from yellow to indigo.
Autumn belongs to philosophers bewildered.

When they see leaves falling and flowers fade,
They start to meditate on the existential crisis.
If spring breeze cut sparrows' tails,
Who brings down those falling and fallen leaves?

Autumn will be possessed by poet,
Since they all claim to be her master.
Joyfulness or melancholy as they beget,
They simply want to chant.

Autumn does not come to me,
But I go to hug her in a fog.

金秋

金秋妙手胜莫奈,
毕加索亦不能盖。
叶色绘以黄靛彩,
秋之哲思莫能猜。

叶落花凋眼前见,
常人生死扰心间。
二月燕尾春风剪,
萧萧落叶听谁言?

诗人独占美金秋,
自诩能为巧心手。
言欢悲秋抒喜愁,
吟诗作赋上心头。

秋日漠然未相睬,
我入雾霭拥入怀。

19 Gingko

When butterflies die out in autumn,
I see golden butterflies a lot of them in our garden,
Floating in the air and flying with the wind.
They are leaves of a special kind.

Gingko, you are there,
When other leaves have fallen.
You turn to be golden,
Decorating woods with splendor and grandeur.

Your leaves take the shape
Of my favorite folding fans,
Hanging leisurely in clusters
Or descending slowly with a drift.

Only China owns you so preciously.
Your golden complexions brighten my sight joyfully.

银杏

秋日蝶绝径,
金蝶满园飞。
随风逐飞舞,
树叶又一类。

此乃银杏叶,
秋日成金黄。
树叶飘落处,
染成富丽装。

银杏叶其状,
酷似折扇美。
簇簇闲暇挂,
悠悠飘然下。

奇珍吾国享,
金艳亮睛窗。

20 Instinct

A baby cries when he comes to this world,
A bird twitters on a tree branch.
A crocodile swims in a lake and hunts for food.
A Frenchman speaks French.

All these we see,
We call them instinct.
But striving to live on
Might be the greatest instinct.

After birth we seem to have no other choice,
But to live on and endeavor to stay alive.
We eat and sleep, cry and laugh.
Who teaches us all these instinctive actions?

Divinity plays a role
Without being known.

天性

婴孩坠地呱呱哭,
鸟雀枝头唧唧咕。
觅食鼍龙水中渡,
法国洋人说邦茹。

世间所见类此事,
皆以天性称谓之。
奋力求生意念执,
炽烈天性最是此。

为人生来无他径,
为求生存力尽倾。
笑面泪颜伴食寝,
谁人育以此天性?

此举乃是天神意,
秘而不泄此天机。

21 Big Cats About the House

Giles Clark is an expert working in a big cat sanctuary
With a purpose to protect and improve their welfare.
One day he took over a five-day old jaguar cub abandoned
By her mother, left behind so tiny, vulnerable and in ill fare.

Giles welcomed her home and named her Maya.
In the first 24 hours he attended her and broke the barrier.
8 times of bottle feeding and cuddling shortened their distance.
Maya became one of the family members by Giles' assistance.

Giles is just like a father for little Maya and drove her 4 hours to a vet center
To check her mobility and eyesight conditions, seeking for professional treatment.
And thanks to his love and devotion, little Maya grows properly and healthily mature.
He taught her to swim and climbing and prepared her for life in wild nature.

The strong sense of responsibility and mission to preserve big cats
Encourages Giles and his family to devote to the humane rescuing acts.

"巨猫"绕屋

护虎行家克拉克,
一心为虎康且乐。
五日幼虎新拾得,
羸弱身薄母弃舍。

贾斯名其曰玛雅,
越界照拂日无暇。
八往喂抚不觉遐,
玛雅融于贾斯家。

贾护雅如父,久驱往医处。
验其手眼足,寻请专人助。
玛雅茁壮长,因贾心相付。
为复归野属,习泳练上树。

护虎之责心中系,
贾斯携家齐心济。

22 Gardening

As a city dweller, gardening is a luxury.
We live in apartments on a certain floor
In the air, there is no soil.
Fortunately, I have a balcony.

So I decided to buy some pots for flowers.
I planned to get some earth from our garden below,
But it would be awkward, because of something I do not own.
I hesitated whether to dig or not, inappropriate for others.

So I decided to buy soils from Taobao, online shopping.
The black soil is nutritious and promising, satisfactory.
I started to plant in my pot with purchased soil for planting.
The seeds I sow are chrysanthemums and morning glory.

In summer and autumn, I may enjoy their splendid blossom,
Watching them grow is now my reward in bosom.

空中花园

城中园艺实可贵,
身居广厦一层内,
触顶高空无土肥,
幸有阳台供栽培。

几盆花株市上鬻,
园中土壤欲私取。
然非我土心生虑,
踌躇终觉非善举。

决以淘宝网购土,
黑土饶沃心满足。
买得新土盆中覆,
播下朝颜与菊属。

秋日花开赏其美,
望其生长心领馈。

23 I Stand Where Peach Blossoms Bloom

I stand where peach blossoms bloom
And I imagine myself to be a poet,
Raising a brush to eulogize such beauty.
The pinkish fairy stands so elegant and gracefully beside the river,
Foreboding her master's coming.

I stand where peach blossoms bloom,
And I imagine myself to be a singer,
Opening my mouth to sing a melody
Which best fits the blossom's rhythm and beat,
Attracting bees and butterflies to join the coming of spring.

The cloud in the sky longs for the splendid hue to clothe.
The flowers are in blossom to compete for beauty.

在那桃花盛开的地方

彳亍在盛开的桃花下,
我仿佛成了花下墨客,
尽情挥毫歌颂桃花之美,
淡粉仙女优雅立在河边,
预感到主人的来临。

漫步在盛开的桃花下,
我仿佛成了花下歌者,
开喉唱响天籁,
伴着桃花的旋律与节拍,
引来万千蝴蝶与蜜蜂加入初春的交响乐。

天上白云渴望身着完美色调,
百花开放,争妍斗丽。

24 Sowing Seeds

These look like tiny balls, black and brown,
But they are not ordinary small balls.
These are flower seeds with huge power
Which makes beautiful blossoms in the falls.

I sowed them in the black soil
In my little pot,
Expecting every day that
Some sprouts pop up tall.

A seed broods of life.
A seed brings about hope.
I walk not alone by myself,
But surrounded with kinsmen and hope.

In the fall I may enjoy beautiful blossom.
Life again will be exhilarated in my bosom.

播种

这些花籽犹如小小的球,黑黑的,
　灰灰的,
但它们不是普通的小球;
它们是充满生机的花籽,
在秋天结满动人的鲜花。

我将它们种在黑黑的土壤,
在我那小小的花盆;
一天天地期盼,
幼芽破土而出。

小小一粒种带来了生命,
小小一粒种带来了希望。
我不是孤独前行,
而是被亲人和希望包围。

秋天我将欣赏美丽的花朵,
我的花里生命涌动。

25 Golden Fish Among Lotus Leaves

The tranquility on the surface is suddenly broken
By a flock of golden fish coming up to breathe.
Or else they are hungry and want to hunt for food,
Frolicking among the lotus leaves hither and thither.

The green lotus leaves are round and relaxing in water,
Trembling a little by a gentle gust of wind or the swimming fish.
The red golden fish hide below them and play wherever
My pond is all alive with view and life's relish.

莲间金鱼

水面如镜骤然破,
争气金鳞结一伙,
或为饱腹寻一嘬,
莲下叶间觅而躲。

莲叶清心如碧盘,
游鱼甩尾随风颤。
叶下金鳞嬉闹欢,
蓬勃池景最赏玩。

26 My Acrobatic Fish

A huge jar with Chinese painting of lotus I bought
In which I shall raise some gold fish I thought.
Six of them, gorgeous and cute went into the jar one day.
A very rich woman I became and felt merry and gay.

Boss, Second, Red Hood, Peanut, Dragon Beard and Tiny,
I named each of them by my simple observation arbitrary.
Boss has the largest size and Second has the second;
Red Hood is all white with a red hood and red tail behind.

Dragon Beard and Tiny are most shy and timid,
But before long they got along very well and frolicked.
My footsteps to the jar make them hilarious.
Each raises their head for their due meal joyous.

Each time after being fed, Dragon Beard makes a somersault
    backward,
Winning my applauds and laughter and hurray, both are equally
    rewarded.

吾养巧技金鳞

莲纹硕罐购于市,
蓄几金鳞成我思。
千金六玉入雅瓷,
裕裕欢喜溢心池。

老大老二小红帽,花生龙须小不点,
信手取名别其态。
老大丰姿胜老二,
素身红帽首尾丹。

龙须不点最羞怯,
片刻共嬉无不谐。
步履稍近众捧腹,
争相仰首把食接。

每每饱餐后,龙须翻跟斗。
欢呼且抚手,双双得赏厚。

27 Golden Lake and Golden Mean

Yutang[1] is teaching me the golden mean for a reasonable man
On the cruise of the golden[2] lake,
When I am holding a fan
To get rid of my headache.

The sublime ordained Noah to make his ark three stories.
By coincidence I saw three geese
On the shoal resting their heads
Underneath the sands.

The spring of the golden lake sounds
And the caves in walls hide
Ancient mysteries from the sublime
To whoever wonders.

The doctrine is divine,
But the lake is not golden.

---

1. Yutang: Mr. Lin Yutang. I am reading his book entitled *My Country and My People*.
2. The golden mean is the Chinese ancient idea of being a mediocre.

金湖之旅与中庸之道

大金湖面游船上
手持蒲扇摇一摇
避暑乘凉驱头疼
语堂讲论中庸道

挪亚授命造方舟
三层上下救生灵
偶见浅滩三只鹅
把头埋于砂石中

听闻湖中泉水声
崖壁洞穴奥秘多
古时传说或许真
无人得以揣摩透

经文教训出神谕
大金湖却非是金

28 Sun Flowers

Roses, lilies and daffodils, I have received from friends,
But sun flowers this time from a student in a surprise.
It is already eleven days past the Teacher's Day.
While a student still remembers me as a good mentor and friend,
It reassures my choice of being a teacher for time and freedom's sake.

He waited outside my classroom for greeting me.
I taught him three years ago and encouraged him to pursue his dream
To enlist as a soldier and be trained for consecutive two years.
He was uncertain and hesitating for a while at that time,
And came to discuss it with me several times after class.

When he joined the army and returned two years later,
A brand new person shining with confidence, majesty and dignity.
He came to see me and told me how grateful he was
For the encouragement and confirmation of the right choice.
He became a better he and that's what I have been expecting.

If I can be the sunflowers' sunshine one day,
Let it be.

向日葵

朋友送给过我玫瑰、睡莲和水仙,
但这次向日葵是我学生给我的惊喜。
教师节已经过去了十一天,
然而有一个学生仍然记得我是良师益友,
它使我因宽松自由选择做老师而感到心安。

他等在教室外面准备送上他平安归来的问候。
三年前我教导他、鼓励他追逐梦想
入伍从军并且连续地训练两年,
那时他犹豫而彷徨,
课后他和我谈论过数次。

当他从军两年后归来,
焕然一新的他闪烁着自信、威严、高贵的光芒。
来看望我的他,表达了他的感激之情,
鼓励和支持他做出正确抉择,
如今的他更加优秀,这也是我所期待的。

如果哪一天我成为照耀向日葵的阳光,
那就快乐地成为那道阳光吧!

29 Autumn

When autumn wind blows,

The maple leaves are dyed red overnight.

A splendid mount view!

秋

一夜秋风起,
满山遍野枫叶红,
更添山色丽!

30 Night

Will there really be a "night"?
Is there such a thing as "day"?
Could I see it from the Everest?
If I were as tall as a giant?

Has it feet like a kitten?
So that it steals into my room without a noise?
Could I have it written
In my poem as a choice?

In the darkness of the night,
Some scholars ponder over it.
Why should the night veil everything pale?
What if day does not come for a while?

Night and day should be in their season.
I believe that I come to being for a reason.

夜

何为夜?
何为昼?
从喜马拉雅能见否?
若高如巨人能见否?

昼夜有狸猫的双脚么?
潜入陋室而悄无声息?
小女入诗可否?
斗胆述说昼夜?

在夜的幕布下,
学者深思悠远。
夜帐万物苍茫,
曙光不临何如?

昼夜轮转而不息,
吾度此生而何为。

31 Sky: My Primer Book

I cannot remember the first book
I read in my life.
It must be the singing brook
Or the skies azure with clouds like anaglyph.

On my way to and from school,
I always gazed with my big eyes at the sky.
The azure firmament entrusted me with infinite reverie.
The heavens of blue sometimes turned into boundless seas.

And I saw myself as a tiny tropical fish,
Swimming carefree within its boundary freely.
The ocean was my mother and the heaven my father,
I was embraced and beloved infinitely and bounteously.

And when I was tired of swimming under the ocean deep,
I emerged as an eagle to explore the expanse of the universe.

儿时看"天"书

所读能记否
人生第一书？
欢唱之溪流，
天云如浮雕。

往返于校园，
常时凝望天。
穹宇使我慕，
蔚蓝成大海。

吾如小鱼儿
遨游于其中，
海母与天父
拥爱享不尽。

倦入海底时，
化作鹰上腾。

32 Nature

The summer drops cheer my hair;
The autumn drizzle cools the air;
Winter sneaks in a flash;
Spring is never too far away from my wish.

Nature, a gentle mother
Makes the softest conversation
To a meek heart however
Restless in a metropolis frustration.

Her voice among the valleys
Incites the profoundest prayer
Of the explorer who conveys
A heart-felt reverence to the Maker.

With infinite affection and infinite care,
Her golden finger makes the sky glare.

自然

夏露沐青丝,
秋雨润躁暑,
冬凛悄然至,
春暖期似许。

自然亲如母,
耳畔诉心语。
处世不得志,
闻听求进取。

幽谷涓涓流,
敬慕深祈祷。
愈探愈感悟,
造化值得敬。

点指穹苍红,
眷爱及永恒。

Part II

Life 生活点滴

1 A Debt to Life

The snowflakes fly outside my window
Like cotton wool frolicking
From heaven falls down my favorite marshmallow
Here and there floating.

I am in a warm room reading,
Wondering if outside there is still someone waiting
For food and warm clothing.
What a blessing I am in lack of nothing!

A debt I owe life
For the breathing and embracing.
Can I pay you back, life
With whatever working?

To love and be loved,
Life is a blessing for the beloved.

生活之恩

雪花窗外飘,
如棉絮嬉闹。
儿时棉糖降,
四处轻飞舞。

书斋读书忙,
衣食尽无忧。
心系寒冬中,
路有饥寒者。

生活之恩欠,
康健安好享。
何德何能来,
报此生之福?

爱与被爱着,
蒙爱享福乐。

2 Love Is Free

I wanted to be a good girl
So that my mom could love me more.
I made efforts to behave well
So that all could love me more.

Yet life has told me silently
Love is generous and free.
There is no need to earn it stubbornly.
Travail is in vain to a certain degree.

The son is always the sun of the family,
And I am a planet circling around invisibly.
Parental love always goes to the younger kid.
Striving is fruitless and no good.

Love is free and magnanimous,
So I shall be big-hearted and bounteous.

爱本无价

我想做个好女孩,
母亲就会更爱我。
努力表现好一些,
众人就会更爱我。

生活默默告诉我,
爱是慷慨又无私。
固执努力不能得,
劳力争取是枉然。

儿子总会成宠儿,
如星捧月成中心。
父母更宠家幺儿,
竭力争宠无果效。

爱本无价非争取,
吾需宽广吾胸怀。

3 Country Dwellers and City Dwellers

The country dwellers came to the city for their livelihood,
Doing some small business is the best one among umpteen choices,
Peddling vegetables and eggs in the neighborhood,
And city dwellers all of a sudden have more new neighbors.

The vegetable supers are cozy and harmonious,
Accessible to every citizen living in the same community.
City dwellers love to visit them quite often at their liberty.
They chat and gossip and become acquaintances.

The integration is subtle and unconscious.
In the Spring Festival the country dwellers say goodbye to the city dwellers.
To go back to their hometowns and city dwellers
Feel so sad and feel at a loss of valuable friends.

Fraternity is no longer very far away from us.
The time you are willing you obtain from others.

城里郊外

乡民入城谋生计,
小本生意为上乘。
水果生鲜邻里售,
市民增添新邻居。

小店温馨又和睦,
近在咫尺叫便利。
市民自由随时逛,
城乡人民成一家。

日益融合悄悄然,
新春乡民返故里。
辞别镇民来年见,
城成空城显冷清。

兄弟友爱非天边,
心愿即生朋友情。

4 An Elegant Lady

She is my Korean tutor, an elegant lady,
Always beams radiant smile on her face,
Affable and approachable like space,
Always encourages me and speaks gently.

12 years ago there was a speech contest,
She tutored me to be a better speaker than anyone else.
I was so grateful and she was contented with my success.
She was just like my mother whom most I trust.

She brought me to swimming, to dining, and to her home
With caring warmth and sound advice in life's adversity.
She prayed for me and read me poems in English.
She is beautiful, kind and most of all, mother-like.

I miss my birth-mother, who has long forsaken me.
Fortunately, the winged seraphs send her to love and care for me.

所谓伊人

伊人倾身授韩文,
沁笑容光彩照人。
和蔼可亲比浩瀚,
柔声鼓劲似清尘。

恩情春秋十二载,
授我以渔胜擂台。
感激涕零报欣慰,
信之如母投以怀。

戏水共宴登门面,
温情忠谏益终身。
祈福吟诗西文里,
淑婉美丽母相生。

生母撒手惜早去,
幸得伊人携爱生。
天自有情降怜人,
六翼天使护拂身。

5 Ode to Fruits

—To name two dozen and two fruits to my son

All say,

"An apple a day keeps the doctor away."

And I will say,

"A fruit a day keeps the clinic away."

Kumquat, loquat, carambola,

Pomegranate, shaddock, papaya,

Plum, peach and pear,

Lychee, longan and mango,

Coconut, durian and persimmon,

Cherry, strawberry, and lemon,

Grape, kiwi, and dragon;

What else don't you have?

Ah, apple, orange and banana,

Hami melon, watermelon, here you are!

水果颂

——为教我儿水果26种,今日写下《水果颂》

人都说:
"一天一苹果,医生远离你。"
我就说:
"一天一水果,医院离你远。"

金橘、枇杷和黄桃,
石榴、柚子与木瓜,
李子、桃子和生梨,
荔枝、龙眼与芒果,

椰子、榴莲与柿子,
樱桃、草莓加柠檬,
葡萄、猕猴与火龙,
还有什么没吃着?

啊,苹果、橘子与香蕉,
西瓜哈密瓜,全都给你啦!

6 Sealed with Three Kisses

He cannot keep his eyes off me,
While I like to look at him in his face and smile.
He cooked delicious food for me to taste, gee,
While I tried to take him looking around the city aisle.

He worships freedom and is frightened
By the bondage of marriage.
Many a man would dodge
Considering a relationship to be fastened.

Let's just seal each other's love
By three kisses, I recommended voluntarily.
One for love, two for care and three for visiting your home.
Is it too much to ask? I wondered ambiguously.

Deal and the deal is sealed
With three kisses for a feel of beloved.

三吻之诺

君情脉脉目流连,
卿谊眈眈迷笑颜。
烹龙庖凤食指动,
串街走巷踏环城。

郎本桀骜慕逍遥,
恐为连理缚折腰。
红尘众客皆迟悯,
婚书一纸葬离草。

秋水为证誓情盟,
三吻以诺定终生。
唯爱永济共四壁,
恐惊雁去思绪纷。

结发为契三吻印,
碧落黄泉情独钟。

7 Sharing

The sharing bicycles renewed the city view.
Wherever you go, the city looks different and new.
The blue-and-white Hello-Bike and the greenish Didi-Bike
Make people love to take more photos.

I hold the truth that if you really love the idea of sharing,
You should love people first with a genuine love,
And care for their life: how they live—
Their health, food, housing and their feeling.

When you share your money with whom you love,
Wonders may happen and you will be more than happy.
I am always pleased that I am economically wealthy,
But actually I own nothing but my family and my love.

Sharing your heart and love with your beloved.
Be generous in using your wealth and wisdom alike.

共享

共享单车焕城新，
大街小巷异彩缤。
蓝白哈啰青桔滴，
流连在路快门频。

念念若享同用情，
切切必先心满馨。
状何生活与生计，
健康温饱与悲欣。

共享汝爱以汝财，
奇迹恍现喜望外。
自足财政幸知运，
除却家馨乌有云。

此心彼愿与伊共，
慷慨财智散若同。

8 Tranquility

Hushed are the crowds, and still their stirring upon the evening gloom,

Not even a zephyr wanders through my window with a murmuring sound,

Only the clock on the wall ticks louder and louder in the bedroom,

On my life journey, many a time I enjoy tranquility around.

I hear myself breathing joyously as a new-born baby,

I listen to every sound with an ear of curiosity,

The drop of water from a tap and a stroke of the string,

The music from the radio and the resounding of the telephone ring.

The weeping of a child and the laugh of a man,

The whistling of the wind and the flowing of a brook,

The rumbling of the thunder and the giggling of an anchorwoman,

In stillness I hear more and more than to write a book.

A madding crowd I try to keep away from,

A tranquil but rich and carefree self I keep in my room.

那刻宁静

日昏人静灯影幢,
西风浅默过人窗。
卧房墙鸣钟漏响,
悦然数寂闻八方。

吞吐声息赤子忻,
侧耳觑然尽收听。
龙头滴答拨弦韫,
电台音乐空荡铃。

孩啼抚掌男声笑,
低语野风溅河流。
闷雷沉天银铃娇,
危坐如面说书人。

沉浮疲倦远痴狂,
宁静无虑善围身。

9 Is It Too Old to Bear A Child?

Oh, thou with delicate tender and loveliness,
Please come to my womb and I await you—
My baby my dream darling and my happiness!
How amazing if you come to my universe thank-you!

Young couples are not well-prepared for a new-born baby.
They themselves are like-babies to be cared for.
Middle aged folks are confronted with a dilemma probably
Whether to have a second child whom they shall be responsible for.

A woman will never be too old to bear a child,
If she loves life and herself enough, since a new-born baby is a gift
From the Almighty and the whole family will take care of it with a shift.
Parents' share is indefatigable toil and unpaid reward.

A new-born creates many a new hope;
A child is a dearer angel from heaven.

孩子,你来晚了吗?

冰肌玉骨赤玲珑,
暖宫柔情候君逢。
心肝梦寐旷以待,
陨玉天降入母怀。

合耄未以迎襁褓,
稚气未脱本年少。
不惑窘遇抉择苦,
仲子与否再育人。

红颜永驻沃土丰,
恋世自重初诞圣。
恩泽举家交拂照,
不辞辛劳无私报。

携福新愿落人间,
白衣化羽自天堂。

10 Stories

When heart with heart in concord beats,

Love is there.

When smile with smile in harmony confronts,

Affection is there.

When eye to eye in acquiesce sees,

Understanding is there.

When face to face in person meets,

A story happens there.

Life is a stage

Where everyone plays a role on it.

When time flies by the age,

The audience are still obsessed with it.

Love, affection, understanding and stories occur.

Our memory and vision begin to blur.

佳话人间

心相印共振,
爱悄自发生。
笑沁眸流转,
惺惺扫情弦。

沉香秋波陷,
明镜照不宣。
邂逅解心猿,
佳话萍水成。

人生如戏台,
唱罢方登场。
流年似水过,
观客意犹饶。

西窗烛未剪,
目眩忆浮沉。

清雅绝尘
庚子秋月
麦子

11 Lost Things and Friends

I always mourned when I lost something mine,
As if that something was an old friend divine.
Though the value was very little
Of which I could not prattle.

The long attachment makes it special
In the memory sequential.
It creates such a feeling,
Quite like in the human dealing.

A friend lost when I was not heeding,
His value astounding,
When I do not care much about,
He's already stepped out.

None of the things or friends are mine.
I shall not well up all fine.

失物与故人

我素潸然为物失，
如丧挚友故连枝。
价廉无以足挂齿，
义浓却难报之嗤。

年华似水情似织，
如珠含蚌粒粒殊。
敝物愫深心相系，
尘世往来亦如斯。

轻狂年少不纳谏，
失友谆谆掷地言。
不知悔兮睨自若，
回首伊已没阑珊。

失物故人皆不再，
彼情彼景不复来。

12 Library

A forlorn child is left alone,
But for the kinsmen of the shelf.
Gee, a day is not so long
That time flies itself.

As cold water quenches
The weary traveler's thirst,
So books bring boon towards
A beloved double first.

In a haven of the unknown
Kingdom of knowledge,
A library is a heaven
For a child of seven.

A library is both a heaven and haven,
Providing a shelter safe for children.

图书馆

形单影不愁,
眷属满书楼。
白日度如秒,
时分纸间流。

恰似掬水凉,
羁旅解涸乏。
书籍携福音,
桃李降甘霖。

未知之港湾,
学识之国寰。
于小儿七岁,
书阁正蓬莱。

庇离尘世扰,
稚子乐安遥。

13 Playing Basketball

The basketball is bouncing, bouncing and bouncing.
My heart keeps dancing, dancing and dancing.
The playground is tossing like a sea wave,
You and I start weaving our unsophisticated love.

So handsome, slim and versatile,
Nimble, natural and you smile.
I cannot keep my eyes off you,
Asking the Maker what I should do with you.

"Life is like a box of chocolate,
No one ever knows what he will get."
The ball keeps bouncing, bouncing and bouncing,
I carry on shooting, shooting and shooting.

My life seems to be twice-born and loving,
"Immortality starts with love," the answer goes on reverberating.

打篮球

篮球横纵东西弹,
我心忐忑上下窜。
无边赛场如浪翻,
你我真爱织不断。

英俊,精壮,万事通晓,
敏捷,自然,是你的笑。
一眼不见心不宁,
急求造化捎我心。

"生活如盒巧克力,
无人能解其中密"。
篮球跃动不曾息,
我与投篮不分离。

我的生命涅槃于滚滚爱河,
"爱即永生",余音响天彻。

14 The London Conflagration

Last week a conflagration broke out at a sudden
In a building in London,
Despairingly with its devastation,
At a speed of spreading and destruction.

As fire and flood commiserates with nobody,
So does nature show any sympathy for the weaklings.
The law of the survival of the fittest exactly
Drives parents mad to strengthen their seedlings.

Children, like cattle and herd are forced to fight
For the scarcity of food and victual provision.
"Spare the rod, spoil the child" brings down many a giant.
So to ask, "Where comes success and succession?"

The conflagration swallowed the building,
Yet compelling strangles our seedlings.

伦敦烈火

上周的烈火爆发于一瞬,
就在一楼宇中就在伦敦。
疯狂绝望地吞噬了一切,
潮鸣电掣般将所及毁灭。

烈火与灼浪毫无怜悯,
自然对弱者绝不同情。
适者生存的法则如钢,
迫使父母逼孩子变强。

如牛犊牧群的孩子们被推向战场,
为紧张稀缺的食物供给剑拔弩张。
"子不打不成器"扼杀了多少巨人,
只问:"怎有功成,何来传承?"

熊熊的烈火已将大楼吞噬一空,
强制的枷锁正勒死我们的孩童。

15 Connection

A simple idea of connection creates the legend of Facebook,
An earnest friend urges me to join a lunch party on a hot summer day,
Life with a purpose is worth seeking,
Amiability and affability are goodness too rare to spare.

To live is to be connected,
To contribute is to have something to give,
To create meaning and purpose for others
Is sublime and idealistic.

Life is hard and difficult for all.
To suffer, to endure and to be exercised in travail.
Love is the panacea for all pains and sufferings
Without which life is like hell.

No one can live alone,
But all are connected.
Better be closely associated with the good,
But keep far away from the evil.

A bond of friendship forged is as priceless as rubies,
And our happiness can be counted as forever endless.

心有所系

一丝相连之念成就脸书的传奇，
炎夏午宴之邀承载挚友的真意。
值得追寻的是以目标为引的生活，
罕而珍贵的是亲切而友善的心魄。

生，乃心有所系；
献，即以物相济。
心载他人而相与游舫，
何其崇高又多么理想。

生活使你困苦又令我窘迫，
去忍受，去经历，去受阵痛的折磨，
一切痛，一切苦，终被爱化作云沫，
如炼狱，如地府，是没有爱的生活。

无人能孤独一生，
世间皆比屋连甍。
近朱者赤故广结善缘，
近墨者黑故与其疏远。

友谊如连城红玉，
快乐将滚滚相续。

16 Melancholy

One of my former students dropped
Out of law school because of melancholy,
Feeling disconnected and depressed
Is considered to be the main cause of the malady.

Technology and automation
Are eliminating many jobs.
More people are feeling depression,
Trying to fill a vacant void with sobs.

To be or not to be
Is no longer Hamlet's soliloquy.
Many people are living
In poverty and loneliness.

Forlorn souls yearn for care and love,
And love alone can cure melancholy.

心愁

我一门生骤辍学，
苦海灌心弃法学。
只身孤岛无所寄，
终致病入膏肓绝。

技术携以自动化，
千行万业皆免罢。
众人方受千斤压，
默然以泪填心乏。

生存乎抑或亡乎，
无复哈姆莱特之独述。
人间众人只身处，
箪食瓢饮独孤苦。

见弃孤魂乞关怀，
唯有大爱散心霾。

17 Save Our Children

A nine-year-old lost her mother's phone in the snow.
In great fury, she wrapped up her son with tapes,
And beat him to death, as we know.
How desperate she could be, yet my heart breaks.

If I can save one child like this from being slaughtered,
I shall not live in vain.
If I can stop one unqualified mother to give birth to a child,
I shall not live in vain.

Children are gifts from heaven,
But we either spoil them or kill them,
Without knowing our own sins,
And deceiving our own conscience.

Save the children,
And set them free to Eden.

救救孩童

茫茫白雪九岁小童遗手机，
忿忿怒火其母布条捆腿臂。
人尽知晓幼童受虐终至死，
我心悯叹其母绝情竟如此。

能使孩童免此难，
我觉此生不徒然。
能止莽妇肆生养，
我觉此生亦无憾。

纯稚孩童天所赠，
娇惯凌虐毁其生。
罪尤过错不自问，
自欺不罢还欺人。

无邪孩童盼得救，
伊甸乐园尽自由。

18 Food Got Burnt

A smoke smothered and smelt
Into my study
All of a sudden,
And I was panicked.

I had started to steam
Some vegetables and eggs
On the gas,
But I fell into a trance.

Not until the pungent smoke
Roused me up,
Did I joke at
My foolish forgetfulness.

Burnt, fortunately, was the food,
But not my mood.

污馐记

袅香萤窗淑,
鼻翕忽焦苦。
举首呆木鸡,
浓烟惊满目。

蒸又熟几度,
水汽弄蛋蔬。
弃置厨灶去,
神恍九天惚。

大梦如初醒,
刺鼻滚烟雾。
方嘲白日疏,
健忘与书缚。

叹惋珍馐污,
却幸静如故。

19 The Tune in Thee

When I listen to a song,
I feel I like the lyric and the melody,
So I hum with the singer at the same tempo.
I sing along and feel happy.

For several days I hum the same melody,
Singing the very song as if I am still listening to the tune.
The program is not in the air,
But the tune is on my mind.

It is a happy tune and slow melody.
I feel like singing with the same melody.
Humming the same story once more
Makes me nostalgic and suffer more.

It is not a tune in the air,
But the tune in thee.

心头的旋律

空耳闻丝篁,
丹心悦词律。
击节随伶唱,
释然共乐章。

萦魂曲三日,
绕梁淌口出。
无音未见韵,
闭目谱自生。

千回调轻悠,
同击春水筹。
往事再频首,
来者泪已流。

莫问此歌何处有,
只道旋律在心头。

20 Recalling All the Good Times in No. 3 Girls' Middle School

When the birthday song was hummed melodious,

Where are you, my friend?

I reserved your seat always

Which used to be decorated splendid.

A period of journey of my prime was accompanied by you.

You and I had accompanied each other like body and shadow.

You and I had squabbled and bickered with sorrow.

You and I, however, had loved each other so dearly.

The sea and sky had witnessed

Our laughter and cheering sound.

The middle school days were so unforgettable.

Merry talks and songs were ubiquitous and memorable.

How transient life is and friendship priceless,

But all are preserved in my poem timeless.

忆市三女中

当生日歌响起的时候，
你在哪里，我的友人？
朋友的坐席为你留起，
那里曾因你蓬荜生辉。

一段人生曾有你陪伴，
我们形影不离过；
我们嬉戏打闹过；
我们彼此相爱过。

大海和天空见证了
我们的欢声与笑语；
中学时代令我难忘，
歌声与微笑常相伴。

生命短暂友情无价——
在我的诗里永存留——

21 A Miraculous Reunion

Two middle school classmates departed two dozen and three years ago,
Today they are meeting each other once again for a get-together.
From two opposite halves of the globe like a moving photo.
One never knows how excited and wondrous life could be for each other.

Holly and Oliver are sister and brother.
They love each other.
The two of them are my friend Mary's children.
They look gorgeous and foreign.

I am proud of Mary, Holly and Oliver,
The three of them are like special gifts from heaven.
In my birthday month, I find it a special favor from the Father,
Who loves me most and bears me in his bosom and haven.

Mary, I bless you with my heart, soul and mind,
Wishing you the best for the rest of your life behind.

重逢

庠却碧玉二七春,
重忘聚首几时分。
舆图穷叠天涯奔,
鲲鹏偃息海角逢。

霍莉手足奥利弗,
形影不离嬉相逐。
吾友玛丽令爱郎,
异域风度玉琢相。

亲子我见喜为骄,
承天应物如三宝。
寿月添福自其父,
拥怀若港意难蒙。

全心全意聚精魂,
伊人安好永晴天。

22 Love, Pity and Mercy

Can I see a falling tear
And not feel the sorrow's share?
Then I am without love.

Can I see a dog's leg broken
And not concern about his sleeping den?
Then I am without pity.

Can I see another human being poverty-stricken
And not worry about his fate conscience-stricken?
Then I am without mercy.

Love, pity and mercy,
These are the common bonds knitting our society,
Without which it goes into bankruptcy.

爱、怜与慈悲

目视泪珠坠,
如何不心碎?
悲恸呼应醉,
情谓爱相随。

路遇跛腿犬,
如何不心悬?
忧其夜归宿,
同情并蒂莲。

见人穷潦倒,
如何不心操?
愧怍蚕舛命,
慈悲逢时到。

爱怜与慈悲,
牵系众生最。
彼心与此愿,
缺一沦永夜。

23 Too Poor to Look Down Upon Money-Making

Many a senior student goes to their internship.
Few attendants appear in due classes.
In the future society graduates are seeking for their membership.
Job-hunting is no easy and competition is fierce.

I cannot tell my students money is not that important in life
To become an anti-conscience liar against my own belief.
Almost every professorship around me is busy making either profit or a fame.
In our curriculum what is the purpose of a profession is not within the frame.

Life is hard and many are from an average family.
To dream big and determine to change the world's possibility
Is not a mistake but maybe not so real nor worthy.
We are just too poor to despise money-making mentality.

To rid poverty fighting for a fortune is the only way out.
That is why we live and long for a new start out.

关于金钱

门生渐稀求仕初,
人迹罕至学知途。
指日出师寻归处,
千军渡桥道踌躇。

利禄难齿过眼烟,
违心莫背志诳言。
追名逐利先生常,
教义不见程未彰。

世事艰阻家道庸,
鸿鹄志平天下同。
齿少心锐空无凭,
清高作态断米粮。

贫困唯靠奋发破,
致富为生启前程。

24 One Girl's Doll Is Another's Devil

All the world is celebrating the Mother's Day, a bliss.
Mothers are supposed to be great and selfless,
Loving their children wholehearted.
But I sympathize with those girls maltreated.

In primary school, two of my girlfriends had younger brothers.
Their mothers preferred boys, assigning them to do much housework.
They lived in misery and hatred, lacking in love and care,
Impossible to be grateful to their mothers.

When they grew up, they married sooner,
The only best way to escape from their mothers.
The word "mother" was curst
In their tender and vulnerable hearts.

They themselves determined to be great mothers
To annihilate the dark memories of their own mothers.

招娣

举世贺母涌泉恩，
颂慈娘亲无私忱。
甘露润子身知寸，
吾怜招娣待误生。

同窗双髻姊幼弟，
母催洒扫偏男息。
酸楚苦恨少惜细，
荡然无存报春晖。

花信梅熟秦晋好，
但求身侧离奔逃。
妈字辞藻厄印烙，
闺心易脆见骨伤。

祈誓愿为良母亲，
晦暗迹销聊自慰。

25 The Death of a Centenarian

A centenarian wishes to die.
I cannot understand why.
People say he is just too old.
I listen to his story carefully told.

Scientist as David is of botany,
Born in UK in the breakout of the war.
Life was hard before it was easy.
He left UK for Australia once for all.

He succeeded in his career as a scientist celebrated;
Published papers until the age of a hundred.
But when he could no longer move about,
He wanted to commit suicide and die out.

He flew to Swiss to be rendered euthanasia, a mercy killing.
His death news was pervasive all over the world.
I still wonder if he had known God beforehand, thrilling.
He would have desperately wanted to be saved.

No matter how much he believed in "die with dignity",
I wish I could share with him the message of eternity.
Sad I was in a deep pensive mood,
Hoping to share and testify the love of God.

期颐离世

期颐许鹤登,
众所未解闻。
人道龟已寿,
吾感骥之文。

大卫精百草,
英诞炮火烽。
艰难苦备尝,
赴澳再无程。

科研就名禄,
撰文至灯枯。
气弱力竭尽,
思顾令自诛。

瑞士针一剂,
讣告飞遍地。
必先觊神迹,
撒手淡无疾。

体面先生去,
愿享授终谕。
悲思陷虑重,
共证承恩露。

26 The International Yoga Day

Yoga is just beyond simple physical exercise,
While it is prevailing in gymnasiums.
I thought it was something similar to Taiji,
Slow and being aware of your respiratory qi.

But yoga masters tell us that yoga is more.
It is science and technology for all,
And for all human betterment
With the key idea of harmony and achievement.

The path starts with changing the individual,
If we want to transform the world as a whole,
A larger manifestation of who we are.
We start to change how we think and travel far

Into history and our society to live in peace
With me, our neighbors and the universe.

国际瑜伽日

瑜伽非类动寻常,
健身房内众霓裳。
窃以此物比太极,
徐起吞吐气若沧。

巧师笑言两相旁,
瑜乃科技为生苍。
广罗世间诸福祉,
和得为魂贯中堂。

道之初自个回轮,
渐步晕染定乾坤。
一花一人一世界,
豁然开朗乃鹏程。

古今中外居安泰,
我自比邻至苍穹。

27 On Diet

No one knows when exactly we start to get fatter.
My older friends have all put on a lot of weight,
So it is high time we went on a diet.
Getting fatter surely will not be better.

But why is almost every lady on a diet?
What changes have happened to our living?
Food shortages are still a big problem we are confronting.
Why are we getting fatter and suffer from it quiet?

Losing weight is not as easy as putting it on.
I succeeded once last year by reducing 7 kilos.
However, the winter coldness and a sedentary vacation
Brought my weight back to the original version.

I determine to eat moderately and vegetables once again,
Trying to find that slim and confident me back again.

节食

几何腰赘骤生脂,
长别面圆皆熟识。
节食不待更何时?
横玉堆砌总难宜。

胭脂满城体嫌肪,
潜移默化易餐妆。
重荒饥口犹待哺,
一方天人苦白滂。

脱脂攻坚战难赢,
去年小胜十四斤。
沁骨寒气炕炉暖,
休假久坐重立弹。

均衡膳食多蔬菜,
决意笑傲复窈窕。

28 On Children's Day

On the Children's Day parents and schools gave children presents,
Books, stationeries, toys, clothes or plays to make them happy.
But asked individually, they denied these unnatural untimely gifts.
They say that's not they really want to achieve a decent holiday.

Oh, that poses a dilemma for adults.
Why don't you want those fun things and fancy activities?
No, they really don't want that.
Children shall not lie to their parents.

Then what do they aspire for at such a tender age?
Maybe they do not really know what they want.
Oh, yes they surely do know their hearts' desire and want.
They want company, quality time and parents' care and love language.

Time and company are best presents for our beloved child,
If we mean to cultivate them to be towering fruitful trees, not wild.

儿童节

亲塾庆赠儿童节,
文书器玩衣乐谐。
窃以飞礼非时令,
别有他求正当迭。

长者相觑疑所虑,
何不心悦奇珍趣?
所思所求非所得,
小儿澄澈面椿萱。

翘首稚龄何所盼?
许不自知晦涩甘。
浩如明镜当知数,
哝声切问眷亲畔。

朝夕相伴遗珍宝,
枝繁果硕参天木。

29 On Free Chinese Ink and Wash Painting

In truth of lines and charm of colors,
You do create a beautiful drawing
Of idyllic beauty and tranquility for us
To enjoy and imagine.

I fall in love with traditional
Free Chinese painting of ink.
Water and ink mixed
Give birth to unexpected images wonderful:

The red cherries and dark red leeches,
Yellow loquats and yellowish chicken,
Swimming gold fish and small herring fishes,
Insects, stones and mountains.

In works of painting you can find vivid life.
In life you feel obliged to paint and hold belief.

大写意中国水墨画

用真实的线条和色彩的魅力,
你创造了美丽的画卷。
为我们描绘田园的秀丽与宁静,
让我们怡然自乐浮想联翩。

我爱上中华传统
大写意水墨国画,
调和清水与浓墨,
画出人意外的奇妙意境:

红红的樱桃、深红的荔枝、
黄色的枇杷、嫩黄的小鸡、
游动的金鱼、小青鱼、
昆虫、石头与高山……

画卷中你可以看到栩栩如生的生命,
在生活中你感到作画的冲动和信念。

30 Love Box

There is a love box in your heart.

Do you know its existence?

When it is full you are exuberant;

When it is empty your life will be filled with abhorrence.

Out of the love box,

We speak several love languages.

The language of affirmation,

And the language of appreciation:

The love language in the form of serving action,

Quality time and sending presents.

When you distribute love languages out of your love box;

When in love, you are the most beautiful one in human civilization.

Love box is a magic box:

Out of it comes purity and holiness.

爱之盒

爱匣芝兰注胸扉,
外化知否递心归?
盈者奕奕神采沛,
乏者靡靡厌恨悲。

触景意发爱盒启,
情至浓时絮语蜜。
抚膺旦旦山海誓,
扼腕拳拳琼瑶许。

温声细语化布施,
全心实意馈礼辞。
柔情高光绝穹宇,
开椟告白广人间。

爱盒之妙不可言,
金玉其内圣洁贤。

31   The Declination

When you wanted to say no to my application,
You postponed our meeting for half an hour by message.
And I said it was all right and I could wait.
Half an hour later you phoned to inform cancelling the meeting.

Then you came to your office and relaxed,
Thinking that I must have left.
But I was still secretly waiting out of your expectation perhaps.
I was disappointed not because of the veto of my application.

I was astounded by how you treated me.
Strategies should be used onto enemies but how could you apply it to your colleagues?
When you left I went to knock at the door of the dean.
I heard his voice from inside but the door was not opened.

I thought maybe there was a meeting inside so I waited.
I always heard one person's voice and knocked at the door for several times.
The door was not opened and I waited outside.
Two hours later it was opened and the dean asked if it was I that had knocked…

I was embarrassed and felt like an idiot.
My brain went blank as if I met a tyrant.

拒绝

汝欲辞我议,
推言迟相计。
我表俟之意,
汝曰就此已。

俄而汝归憩,
料我必已离。
不知我仍立,
绝辞非所戚。

汝之待人我惊异,
应敌之计施近已?
我寻执事评其理,
闻声敲门门不启。

盖行要务我候俟,
敲门亦有三五次。
闭门良久我不辞,
门启佯问何人此。

愚不可耐空自窘,
恍然若遇暴君统。

32 The Power of Literature

A mother who was devoted to reading literature came to me,
Asking a favor if I could teach her daughter writing.
Her girl was very international and started creative writing.
Isabella typed on Mother's mobile phone whenever she would agree.

The mother said when she went through life's perplexity,
It was the power of literature and books that she had read sustained her.
One day her soul flew like a bird onto a branch overlooking at her weary body,
Sweating to make a living and empathized her.

"You suffered a lot, my child, but you will be richly rewarded one day!"
Her soul comforted her dreary body, doing some temporary job in a restaurant,
She loved stories, novels, poems and plays she had read during her school days.
They revealed to her: "C'est la vie—life is difficult."

So she firmly believed that literature can nurture her girl best,
Amazed at the fact that Isabella started to create novels at only eight.

文学之力

一酷爱文学的母亲前来,
请求我扬其千金之文采。
国际型女孩将思路打开,
母亲应允及入打字状态。

母亲倾诉她曾经遭遇的生活困苦,
文学之力与饱揽之群书给予支撑。
一日心绪跃上枝头俯瞰疲惫之身,
挥汗如雨为保生活之本,心头一振。

"你受苦了,我的孩子,但终有一天你将得到丰厚的回馈!"
餐厅打工的日子困苦不堪,疲倦之身只有心灵给予安慰。
校园时期品读的故事、小说、诗歌和戏剧是她酷爱之最,
它们向她揭示生活的真谛:这便是人生,如同带刺玫瑰。

她因此坚信文学是给女儿最好的滋养,
惊喜于伊莎贝拉年仅八岁便崭露锋芒。

33 Isabella

Isabella is a genius, a child prodigy.
She is only ten but has travelled around the world already.
She loves London most and is fond of playing with words.
Harry Porter is her favorite novel and she prefers Hogwarts.

When she has her mobile phone in her hand,
She starts to key in words and create stories.
Her language is plain and direct from the perspective of a child,
But interestingly I am attracted by childish innocent fantasies.

Rebecca gave birth to Isabella and claimed to her child:
I am your mother and we are equal with mutual respect.
So please be an adult and revere your parent.
The two of them read and talk and play together like friends.

Rebecca and Isabella came into my life story.
I think it is going to change my personal history.

伊莎贝拉

伊莎贝拉乃神童,
垂髫天下遍周游。
雾都钟情喜弄墨,
巫师世界梦牵魂。

手机在握气神闲,
休笔成章著芸签。
平言直叙稚儿语,
奇思妙想烂漫言。

谆谆其母丽贝卡,
亲子平坐当相庄。
轻熟成长尊父母,
两厢交好共娱议。

结识慈媛幸今生,
润木无声化年轮。

34 Mannerly Neighborhood

The morning call I missed, working in the kitchen.
When I found out, I called back, as a friend reckoned.
It was from a neighbor uncle who was really benevolent.
He brought me some juicy fresh peaches from Wuxi as a gift.

A few months ago, his grandson was going through some interviews.
To enter a famous elementary school isn't easy these days.
He came to me for correcting the child's pronunciation.
How smart the boy was and I loved the kid with great emotion.

For a continuous few weeks I went to their house, a next building,
To help the kid recite his self-introduction poem in English.
A child of six, he talked as a well-educated little gentleman, polished.
A month later, good news came that he was accepted for schooling.

Good neighbors outweigh remote relative.
Good neighbors are best, like one family, acceptive and acquisitive.

贤邻

晨铃错入庖屋繁,
未几回播依友喃。
居邻世叔何慈善,
锡寄水灵蜜桃鲜。

数月逾孙面试迎,
名塾难入小儿竞。
来访纠音解句读,
慧童吾喜爱备伶。

周临彼舍隔邻楼,
导诵外语报家门。
始龀谈吐乱儒生,
三旬喜闻录取成。

远亲不如贤近邻,
海纳如归众所求。

35 In Guilin

River Lijiang is famous for its mountains and rivers,
The reflection and the silhouette view trigger people's imagination.
This mountain looks like an elephant; that one resembles a dolphin mother.
Being told of such images, you feel happy and ready to accept those notions.

However, sometimes I think they are just mountains covered with green trees.
Without imagination mountains are just mountains.
Why people may believe in those gorgeous stories?
It's because they are created to be a wiser species.

Stories are made by humans,
For humans and to be believed by men.
Nature is created by Mother Nature.
Men are made to create more wonders.

Nature is amazing and respectable,
Feeding us with milk, food and dignity.

桂林游

丽江山川天下奇,
倩影旖旎印涟漪。
象纠豚哺似群岳,
巧思妙想欣自期。

时窃腹诽本青峦,
幻灭自娱情何堪。
宁信其有瑰丽传,
是以浪漫智非凡。

故事佳话由人撰,
说与人听为人传。
昆仑造化自鬼斧,
圆首方足添奇古。

惊叹自然肃起敬,
乳辈果腹脊骨尊。

36 A Surgery

The cyst on my neck of the left shoulder
Kept growing and I was informed by the doctor
That I had to go through a surgery to have it cut.
It had the size of a bean and its center was black and tight.

It looked like bursting anytime you pressed on it,
So I was frightened and anxious about the cut.
The surgeon was an old experienced man outstanding
With a rosy face and radiating eyes, smiling.

I was injected anesthetic drugs and lost my feeling.
I saw him with a knife in his hand and fainted.
When I opened my eyes again and successful
Was the surgery and the cyst looked nauseated.

Several stitches were made, afterwards I could not move my head.
Suddenly I felt how fragile and vulnerable life is and lamented.

记手术

左肩渐沉苦囊肿,
附颈日厚求郎中。
将布相告切除了,
豆大珠顶乌岩重。

饱胀欲裂但经触,
胆战心惊危手术。
老手操刀平佼佼,
容光笑面炯炯安。

麻药上头四肢绵,
刀悬阖目渐晕眩。
神回转醒手术毕,
囊肿清离垢滩污。

针缝密痕颅难转,
生灵叹惋易摧折。

37 Metropolitan Loneliness

Behold him, single in the crowd,
Yon solitary metropolitan lad!
Wandering and roaming by himself alone!
Stop here and there, or gently scan.

No brilliant eyes have ever seen
More colorful life than the countryside.
No one tells him that city life is all about fortune,
Breaking the peace of ordinary has-been.

However, in the great multitudes one feels at a loss.
The only thing for sure is alienation or solitariness.
Will no one tell me what he is looking for?
Perhaps the purity of a fountain of love metaphor.

A metropolis is crowded with people from all walks of the society,
Yet hardly is there anyone your bosom friend to share your actuality.

寂寞都市

万千红尘独萧索，
都市漂泊风雨多。
略影浮光芳菲过，
天下无依残灯火。

嫩柳篱桥花飘落，
乡村美景月婆娑。
蓬头垢面长漂泊，
世人皆为名利锁。

茫然无措在京洛，
疏离孤苦都休说。
世事风波求何物，
爱如泉涌暗香陌。

往来金剑绯绸罗，
愁云惨淡心难托。

38 The Story of Pomegranates

A pomegranate is the most amazing fruit in the world.
The golden brownish skin embodies a whole palace inside.
When broken off, a labyrinth of pinkish agates pop into sight.
Who arranges them into such a pattern neat and bright?

In those days when pomegranates were dear and rare,
My 5-year-old son pestered me to go and buy his favorite pomegranate.
I challenged him to spell the word in English correctly then acted.
He repeated the word "pomegranate" in his room for an hour.

Confidently he articulated the word "pomegranate" without a break,
And I kept my promise to go and get him three juicy fresh fruit.
My son's joy was memorable and tremendously innocent.
He broke off the pomegranate and started to count.

The little "rubies" he put in a bowl and swallowed them in a gulp.
That was the very beginning of his memory of words without any help.

石榴记

石榴奇异果中王,
棕金皮下掩其宫。
桃色玛瑙迷人眼,
纵横错落最玲珑。

石榴稀时价更高,
吾儿急欲品其妙。
拼得单词吾方买,
屋中良久把舌绕。

倒背"石榴"亦如流,
吾购三榴多汁肉。
难忘吾儿童真乐,
细数籽肉无一漏。

碗中晶玉珠,一口皆入肚。
吾儿初识词,全然无需助。

39 Happy Teachers' Day

Masters are supposed to propagate ancient doctrines and thoughts,
Teach their students to be good, instruct them in righteousness,
Solve their questions in case they grow up to be good-for-naught,
Impart professional knowledge to their disciples for goodness.

In China there are more than 15 million teachers registered.
I became one of them fortunately a decade and seven years ago.
The biggest boon of being a teacher is staying young minded,
Keeping up with the latest trend and trying hard to crucify the ego.

There are so many teachers in my life who exert great influence
On me, not those who are really articulate, but those
Who cared for me and gave great love to me and touched me
With their words and actions as a model how to be.

Great teachers are rare to meet and influential in one's life.
Happy are teachers who are respected for their steadfast belief.

咏师

师者传道古训蒙,
弟子成器先成人。
解惑授业学有术,
栽桃培李书德承。

华夏西宾册万千,
幸跻列载余一廿。
最喜观念时新异,
山长弄潮日抑谦。

先生枚举过留痕,
非也巧舌亦能言。
悉心爱护涟漪起,
寓教于行心口一。

良师难遇终身益,
欣长但逢矢志尊。

40 The Secrets of Long Life

Who in this world would not want to prolong life?
The secret of a long life is nothing but positive psychology.
Get rid of depression, sadness, sorrow, strife and melancholy,
Instead be thirsty for bliss, felicity, joy, gratification and prosperity.

Calling on me yesterday with her daughter and son,
My bosom friend looked younger than a decade ago and her daughter was really a beauty.
The satisfaction and joy of raising children hardly hidden.
She was totally selfless and ignored young ladies' worries of jobs and obesity.

Children's naïvete and curiosity occupy her mind,
She returns to a child's way of thinking and living.
Smiling and laughing from time to time when eating,
Her life is filled with hope and possibilities undefined.

Children prolong parental life,
By inheriting their spirit and skills.

长寿的秘诀

世人皆求益延年,
长寿秘诀但心宽。
远离哀怒诸烦恼,
渴慕幸福喜安康。

登门知己伴瓦璋,
逆龄十载并蒂芳。
提携安乐溢言表,
玉体无忧事业旷。

懵懂好奇耳目濡,
还童纯善知行初。
眉开眼笑竟时宴,
憧憬无限遍扶苏。

子息再世续终曲,
衣钵继承回永春。

41 A Good Husband Is Hard to Find

When autumn comes it is the season to relish shaddock.
My husband always brings one home for after-dinner dessert.
I acknowledge that good husbands are hard to find for wedlock.
However, I am blessed with a caring and considerate soulmate.

When he sings songs I will sing along with satisfaction.
When he cooks in the kitchen I feel being loved deeply.
The best of all is that he listens to me with all his concentration,
As if I am speaking of things of great value magnificently.

He seldom says he loves me with words and expression.
He told me love is an action beyond articulation.
I disagree and reveal to him the truth:
All women would like to hear that oath.

Two is better than one and love is reciprocating.
We try to love a love that is more than love rewarding.

佳偶难寻

秋意恰浓橘柚红,
官人日归尽飧分。
佳偶难觅况夫婿,
众里寻作温良人。

夫唱妻和击节叹,
郎庖女啖濡沫耽。
最喜君倾闻我道,
如听懿旨晤乐仙。

甜言寡淡蜜语鲜,
振振托辞行胜言。
恕难苟同先生告,
耳鬓厮磨永窈窕。

比翼高飞情相候,
自始琴瑟终白头。

42 A Confession

A cute boy student confessed his secret in class.
I was astonished by his straightforwardness.
He had a lot of talent in language learning,
Being very smart, courageous and outgoing.

In his presentation, he told the whole class candidly
That he was born different and he knew it already.
He was feminine and he said he was gay.
On hearing it, I had no idea where my hands should lay.

An open and unbiased teacher as I am,
I still cannot stop worrying about the student's confession.
What are people going to say about him?
How will his future be influenced by this orientation?

The incorporation of new information help we grow spiritually;
However, can we embrace all diversities graciously and generously?

自白

俏书郎开诚,
率直惊赫然。
横溢语才赋,
皓洋智勇全。

初堂自布公,
天生众不同。
阴柔兴分桃,
手乱无处安。

自觉开明维,
却恐白生悲。
世言何所倦,
康庄殊途催。

暖流护苗长,
北冥百纳无?

43 For Procrastinators

When I feel tired after a day's teaching,
I would keep quiet and listen carefully
To a tiny little voice inside me murmuring:
You deserve to take a rest contentedly.

So I would indulge myself and be sluggish.
What is supposed to be done will be procrastinated.
I put off my jogging plan till tomorrow, foolish.
I comfort myself not to bother writing research papers appointed.

Excuses I created myself cheated myself every day,
When can I be true to myself and make decisions to take action?
Instant gratification, easy and fun busy my day,
When shall I rid the old nonfeasance and lazy approximation?

Procrastination bothers every one of us without a deadline.
Life with a purpose will make all the difference as a lifeline.

致拖延症

授堂终日乏，
沉心空耳挂。
微喃心生絮，
闲惬意自足。

怠己纵横懒，
行所暂搁延。
漫步推明日，
文书置离忧。

藉口欺更少，
真意决断逃。
简适浮碌趣，
又恐惰无为。

拖延苦无期，
望归改终途。

44 In Father's Name

She was admitted to Harvard as an exchange student,
As a Chinese sophomore how demanding and ambitious.
Yet she made it through many years' strains and pains.
In father's name he was really satisfied with her achievement.

Yet in father's name he should preserve his strict streak
To keep calm and quiet about her excellence.
She studies harder and harder without any break.
In father's name he is praying for her transcendence.

A great father's love is such
With few praises but encouraging.
He seldom shows his contentment,
Yet loving and more than often supporting.

In father's name his love is abundant,
His care and concern always affluent.

以父之名

哈佛榄枝伸,
华夏学子琛。
经年寒窗苦,
父傲女所成。

父亦何其敛,
沉默注骄人。
女更日夜修,
父自卓越求。

此乃宏父情,
语鲜意励身。
满欣少流露,
爱浓立山擎。

父爱深涌流,
心底关照厚。

45 The Meaning of Posterity

The richer and more modern young men get,
The less keen are they to get married.
They desire for more freedom and care-free life,
Making their parental generation worried.

To live a single and burden-free life
Becomes many a youth's dream.
Without a spouse or any children,
Me and my world is the real self-esteem.

What will become of the family?
What is the meaning of posterity?
How may a family continue without descendants?
Who will accomplish our country's prosperity?

Our heirs and successors carry on our hope and faith.
All pains and sacrifices will be paid off with their worth.

后浪

青少富渐潮，
灼桃随褪昭。
自在喜无虑，
父辈忧今朝。

独身牵挂了，
少郎魂牵绕。
清侧免子女，
吾身世尊韶。

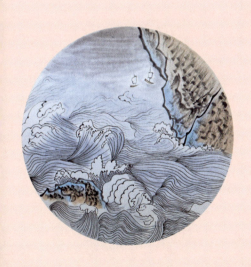

家族通何处，
子嗣意曷图？
后裔尽香火，
家国孰昌延？

后浪承冀志，
血汗许光驰。

46 Thanksgiving

Thank you for giving birth to me, Mum.
Thank you for being very strict with me, Dad.
Thank you for accompanying my childhood, Brother.
Thank you for settling in Shanghai, Grandpa and Grandma, indeed.

Thank you for marrying me, dear.
Thank you for loving me so much.
Thank you for tolerating my hysterical whims.
Thank you for understanding me so much.
Thank you my friends for supporting me so much.

Not only on Thanksgiving am I grateful to you, my Lord.
I thank you always for guiding me to go on with my journey.
I rely on you as my rock, my strength and house of defense.
I thank you always for protecting me from dangers and iniquity.

I give thanks to God, making mention of your goodness,
Remembering without ceasing your deeds of kindness.

感恩

母恩浩荡诞子成,
父爱无疆严律身。
怜弟陪伴幼嬉闹,
庆祖定居扎沪城。

感君共携步婚堂,
幸得郎宠温心房。
抚灭嗔怨无名火,
佳婿益友并肩膛。

谢主隆恩非但日,
戴德永怀明道驰。
固若金汤信强御,
远离苦厄免不公。

叩天拜谢垂恩怜,
终岁毋忘善念念。

47 Ode to Poetry Lovers

There is a conference
Of poetry lovers
Who love poems,
Bearing their dreams.

The art of poetry
Awakens our souls
And heals our maladies.
What matters is artistry.

To feel, to read, and to experience
A poet's life of passion, thinking and doubting;
To suffer, to bliss, and to pay patience
To a poet we respect and share understanding.

Poems feed our hearts with mana
And our bodies with stamina.

诗歌爱好者颂

佳日荟云集,
隽采歌赋词。
好诗难释手,
壮志步星移。

诗歌妙艺精,
醍醐绝顶临。
心疾体病愈,
诗学美意铭。

心感阅体验,
诗人情虑千。
苦乐斯理度,
尊享共联翩。

诗魔滋心力,
曲仙耐体依。

48 Never Say Goodbye to BNU

It was my first time to go to BNU.
To be a teacher has always been my dream.
To go to Beijing is another childhood yearn.
Oh, great leaders and imperial universities!

The campus is colorfully decorated with gingko leaves.
I walked around with exalted awe and happiness.
The sheer size of the library
Overwhelms me speechless.

In the hall of BNU for two days,
Scholars and teachers gather together,
Holding a seminar to discuss poems.
We feel never so closer to each other.

With home-and-abroad poetry in history,
We are so united for the love of poetry.

再会，北师大

初临访北师，
春蚕始梦织。
京都别热念，
人杰校地灵。

碎金纷园缀，
崇敬悦蹒跚。
广厦宏书阁，
惊艳塞语喃。

会堂留双日，
学者荟师集。
研讨论诗意，
相印密相知。

古今韵中外，
情结缘诗联。

49 5:30

It is said that you need
To have a big dream in your mind.
To get up at five thirty
Not because you are thirsty.

If you can get up at five thirty naturally
Without an alarm clock,
What will you do this early in the morning?
Do you want to do creative writing or take a shower?

Five thirty seems to be too early and impossible
For city dwellers to get up,
Unless you have a reason
For accomplishing a vision or mission impossible.

As for me I prefer the fresh air and mind
To get close to the Spirit and new find.

卯时二刻

未旦晨难起,
须怀鸿鹄意。
卯时二刻觉,
口干舌未燥。

神清气自爽,
巧离铜漏宕。
凌晨何充晌?
创作抑沐霜。

时刻早过期,
城居犹未继。
除却别开事,
祈愿务桩毕。

气沁畅胸晏,
魂晤真谛明。

50 Fathers Are More Welcomed

Two neighbors came to my house,
Seeking help and solutions to their families.
As a teacher, I felt much honored and obliged to help,
So we sit down to talk and discuss.

When I inquired into the entire confusion,
They revealed that their children wanted to escape from their mothers.
What a surprise! How sad mothers would be
Who gave birth to and raised them with so many pains.

The prime problem is that mothers are too harsh and push too much.
Their children are suffocating and wish to play truant.
Is all the pressure exerted on kids really for their sake?
Or is it for the sake of parents' vanity or unfulfilled dreams?

Fathers are more welcomed by children, never breastfeeding.
Leniency and understanding are best in educating and befriending.

爸爸更受欢迎

双邻莅舍寒,
求助解家难。
为师欣受命,
促膝共长谈。

纠惑全盘托,
子逆叛母驳。
惊慈何所挫,
生养百般跎。

首祸揠苗驱,
抑窒以辍学。
负重孰体恤?
光宗夙愿虐。

未哺父本亲,
宽量育自近。

51 No Empty Seats in Starbucks

It was nine o'clock on a usual Sunday.
I went to the Starbucks to meet my friend.
Since I was the early arriver, I looked around for a table,
But to my great surprise there was none around.

The only seats left were around a big long table,
While all the small tables were occupied.
More middle aged couples were sitting there.
Some even dozed off and leaned against sofas.

From their conversations I overheard
That there was an examination in Tongji University today.
These parents accompanied their kids here and were anxiously waiting
In Starbucks to kill two hours, a disastrous event for me.

Their kids are their stars of tomorrow.
Where children go there their parents follow.

星巴克满座的一天

寻常浮生已时闲,
咖吧会友常青延。
辰前四顾觅虚位,
讶异惊觉客满帘。

空席独篌长桌央,
对座圆案宾济堂。
秦晋中岁接踵落,
椅榻行眠坐卧茫。

侧耳隙谈漏语闻,
同济大降庠试争。
赴考伴子焦切待,
时辰细走偏我逢。

望子成龙翌星曜,
天涯海角相随尘。

52 Life's Intervals

Who can afford to raise those rich flowers?

Only if you may steal a spring afternoon for tea and leisure.

Life is like a sleep with dreams but no intervals,

Honors and contributions shine upon a guiltless conscience.

浮生若梦眠无暇

花开富贵落谁家,
春日悦窥伴沏茶。
浮生若梦眠无暇,
功德无愧照日华。

53 The 70th National Day

Three score and ten years ago, the red five-starred national flag
Was first raised and fluttering above Tiananmen Square.
Seventy years later, 100,000 people gathered once again
To celebrate our great New China's birthday today.

The same gate that witnessed the vicissitudes of our nation,
Standing magnificently in the center of the city, joyful and most excited,
It saw the military parade upgraded from a low level to an advanced one.
It is the same gate on which our first founding fathers declared liberation.

Workers, peasants, students, army men and people from all walks of the society
Gathered together for a glittering pageantry for the 70th time, singing and dancing.
To prove to the world that we have stood up as a nation and grown stronger.
The firing of the cannon salute declares our prosperity, pride and patriotism.

Seventy years may be a short period of time in the long river of human history,
But for our Chinese people it has been touched with much hardship and victory.

庆新中国70周年华诞

光阴荏苒七十载,熠熠五星红旗在。
天安门前初捧戴,迎风奕奕展神采。
七十昔往今日来,十万儿女相逢再。
普天同庆皆乐恺,祖国华诞入心怀。

昔日城门睹沉浮,
百感欣喜城中腹。
精锐部队添新伍,
开国昭告此宣布。

工农文武千百行,
共聚盛典歌舞昂。
崛起强国向世彰,
爱国豪情随炮扬。

历史长河七十年恍一瞬,
华夏儿女渡艰苦终得胜。

54 A Special Gift

This is the kind of gift you only get from mothers:
A dozen of fresh eggs as a thank-you gift
For my weekly visit and attendance.
Being grateful as well I feel very confident.

On my way back home I started to read
In a subway compartment most crowded.
Coming across an impressive sentence,
I fumbled into my backpack for a marker at once.

All of a sudden, the package with eggs dropped
From my bag onto the compartment floor crushed
With a crisp, sudden and ringing sound,
Rousing people around to my attention.

"Here is a plastic bag, young lady.
These are very fresh and nice eggs."
An elderly woman beside me said,
Rendering me a benevolent smile and a new bag.

特殊的礼物

殊赠独母琛,
鲜卵馈礼彭。
晨昏省亲问,
感慰周计恒。

归途阅笔耕,
厢隙腹背扪。
佳句追难逢,
笺注探顾身。

覆袋惊坠声,
溢包直下沉。
脆响横空亘,
四众瞩经闻。

"小娘予袋封,
鸡子妙新成。"
长妇旁安顿,
慈眉惠施蒙。

55 The Story of the Dark Lady and Her Mum

She wears somber dark fur all over
With glittering yellow eyes.
She looks more elegant and smarter
Than ordinary stray cats.

Her mum is her adopter,
Who did not have the heart to leave her abandoned,
Tiny and pitiful, lonely and uncared
By the sidewalk, ignored and alienated, to suffer.

She took her home, fed and sheltered her daily,
Like a mother attending her own newborn baby.
Her lovingkindness kindled intelligence
Of the kitten with special retrieving skills.

Love creates magic and love repays love.
No earthly reward shall surpass blessings from above.

黑美人

黛袍曳生姿,
金玉盼流瓷。
绰约冰雪智,
脱凡野猫黎。

拾道作母庇,
犹怜何弃离。
芥戚茕无依,
径苦未斜睨。

檐下温饱施,
心悉襁褓慈。
善养福灵至,
巡回异赋识。

神情终归一,
普世报无敌。

56 New Year's Resolution

On the last day of 2019 a friend shared
With me his New Year's resolution—
To lose some weight and to write a book.
How wonderful it is to wish
For something you have long longed for.

My New Year's wish is to achieve something harsh.
There is no need to be in a rush.
Yet with the passage of time like a flash,
When shall I realize a New Year's wish?
In the end, I stop making New Year's resolutions.

Be it fortune to come,
I shall achieve some.

新年愿望

己亥落尾交祈年,
宽衣带来撰书愿。
美谈何妨庄自虔,
心系满怀挂牵念。

吾愿新史治弩鞭,
操之无急蔽恼嫌。
良辰易逝云过烟,
憧憬渐冷终绝缘。

得之我幸悦圆年,
末了心言许得间。

57 My Heart's Ease

My little heart's ease was disturbed by the plague.
An epidemic hectic was spread from a central city.
More than 500 people have been affected, causing a national panic.
The recollection of SARS in 2003 was still vivid in my mind.

At this time of the year, every household was celebrating Spring Festival.
Who would be waiting for a plague's arrival?
The love and eating of seafood was reported to be the culprit.
The virus was said to cause symptoms such as cough and fever.

The worst thing was that Wuhan was blocked.
No people could depart from the city from today.
I pray that the temperature will rise and summer come sooner.
By then the infected will have been cured and away from suffer.

An individual's sickness will largely influence people around.
I pray that all shall be healthy, safe and sound.

我本平静的心湖

骤疾波起乱心湖,
肺疫肆卷霍邦都。
半千尽染举国怖,
前载非典历在目。

家和本度庆春节,
无人先知疫情虐。
海鲜好者负唾弃,
病毒传症嗽风寒。

犹苦武汉固封城,
百姓俱守无人奔。
祈愿回暖夏日至,
患者康复离病苦。

只例扩散一传百,
祝福健康永安泰。

58 The Plight of an Epidemic

Our nation is confronted with an epidemic disease
Which has infected more than 20,000 people.
In this predicament, we can see the difference
Of human heart, selfish or selfless example.

In the plight, some volunteered to go to the front.
Some elevated prices; others donated articles in urgent need.
Some made forgery masks; others quietly transported patient.
Some spread rumors; others encouraged people afraid.

A plight is a battlefield to test every one of us.
A battle distinguishes cowards and heroes.
Some are willing to do good for others;
Others do harm or look on and criticize.

Novel coronavirus is not most fearful indeed,
But a cold, indifferent and apathetic mind.

战"疫"

华夏九州困疫情，
庶民二万染恶疾。
危难险境似开镜，
利己无私显见明。

艰阻请缨赴一线，
有人抬价有人捐。
伪劣护具照劫渡，
诽谤谣言鼓人别。

困窘修罗众人夭，
懦夫英雄见分晓。
贤士助人乐行善，
小人冷眼唯讥诮。

新冠疫情不足惧，
最恐人心淡炎凉。

59 A Dream

When the night is at odds with morning, which is which,
I woke up from my dream.
Casing darkness had I never seen such
Was falling down upon my kingdom.

Within citizens could not breathe
Nor could they eat or sleep.
I managed to fly and flew to the zenith
With a sword I pierced open a gap.

Sunshine peeps in and pours down.
People dance and cheer to welcome dawn.

梦境

晨昏万物朦,
混沌恍惊梦。
乌瘴未所闻,
举国穷追瓮。

黎民口鼻噎,
寝食难昼夜。
乘风唯登临,
挥剑破苍穹。

阳光复亲临,
欢欣迎黎明。

60 The Virtues of Being Quarantined

Being on a lockdown,
I do not feel down.
I prefer to stay indoors,
Feeling free and relaxed always.

Concentration becomes easier.
No thieves nor robbers will haunt a house.
Filled with family members,
My house is my domain.

I become queen of my nutshell.
Lonely not shall I feel.
Infinity is travelled in my mind's eye,
History all but a blink of my eye.

Greek mythology time I would prefer
To go invite the god of fire and thunder,
Scaring and scorching the demons away.
Will bliss and freedom be far way?

隔离之趣

封城不封心,
我心尤欢畅。
室内方寸间,
自由任我行。

心神无二用,
无贼免盗忡。
亲属交相拥,
主宰陋室中。

胡桃匣子王,
无寞扰心房。
神魂永弛漾,
汗青瞬息章。

入潜希腊纷,
往邀火雷神。
魂飞瘟神散,
幸福自由萌。

61 Young and Promising

Under the neon lights,
How I wish to have a place.
While we had some fights,
Love was too hard to face.

Your eyes grew red.
I did not understand.
You were just too fond of me,
Reluctant to put it to an end.

Being young and promising,
I could not humble myself.
Without knowing cherishing,
Our first love was brief.

If I were young and promising again,
I would not have let you taste pain.

年少轻狂

霓虹幻阑珊,
许地少纤尘。
口角过矛盾,
相爱难相诚。

楚楚红潸泪,
惶惶惑我心。
君卿我至深,
何怨掷围城。

年少自轻狂,
桀骜本清高。
珍爱不知物,
情纵始张皇。

如故韶华复,
怎教肝脑涂?

62 A Butterfly's Dream

The butterfly is whispering her dream into my ear.
The breeze is crossing the mountains to seek for home there.
The drizzles awake the sleeping caterpillar and make her smile.
I will knit the butterfly's dream into a kite to fly into the sky.

The butterfly's dream has wings
To the high sky for flying.
I stretch longer the line of my kite,
And draw love on the face of ages' bite.

My heart is the strength of my youthful growth.
Just as a butterfly's wings fluttering in the wind.
The butterfly flies in the wind of my childhood,
Higher and higher into a rainbow of faith.

The butterfly flies and flies into a future castle
To open a window of vision for my youthful whistle.

蝶之梦

风斜入耳蝴蝶梦,
气轻觅去峦山峰。
毛毛虫醒沐雨笑,
蝶梦化织纸鸢翔。

以梦为翼蝶衣漾,
韶华为疆竞翱翔。
添线舞墨风筝远,
赋情弄砚姣容全。

吾心如注灌苗长,
蝴蝶振翅迎风倘。
飞跃山谷幼时梦,
渐高化虹青春芒。

蝶起前落入郭堡,
少郎哨笛踏梦来。

63 A Lovely Child

He has a poetic name.
He has innocent eyes.
He grows tall, yet still a child.
Child as he is, he tries to understand the adult world.

He has rich imagination.
He wants to escape the burden of heavy study
Just like every other peer.
He is a very lovely child.

We should respect their innocence.
We should let them free.
We should make them happy.
We should not push them too hard.

Children are from heaven.
We should all return to children.

孩子来自天堂

名惠赋诗意,
眸清呦鹿啼。
玉树未临风,
懵懂陌迎逢。

烂漫游九神,
破塔远繁纷。
意气类书生,
犹怜我见萌。

纯真值尊重,
桎梏终无痕。
风华本年少,
揠苗助莫衷。

孩童浑天成,
返璞尽归真。

64 Simba and Tutu

"A good heart will always be requited," many people quote.
I saw a kitten meowing sadly on the fence of a nearby park.
It was skinny and had caught some eye disease, unfortunate.
I sympathized it and took it to the veterinarian's clinic.

The vet checked and told me that three days' injection would cure him.
Though the treatment was a little costly, I brought it home with a jocund heart.
If I could help one fainting robin unto his nest again, I should not live in vain.
I felt the heart of Emily Dickinson's heart when she wrote it.

I named the he-kitten Simba as I thought he was very courageous
To call for help from strangers like me and looked like a mini-lion.
To accompany him, I also bought a pet-dog, Tutu, a white Pomeranian,
Fluffy like a snow-white cotton ball, cute with clear and bright eyes.

Within three days, I have got a kitten and a puppy, attaching to each other.
They became innocent playmates and brought me so much unexpected cheer.

辛巴和图图

好人好报常人言,
遇猫幼啼邻园边。
嶙峋瘦骨悲目障,
悯生心来抱投医。

兽医切诊三日药,
疗愈不菲喜迎猫。
倘遇知更助回巢,
艾米莉心幸世昭。

名谓辛巴赞其勇,
幼狮急吼命人从。
又得博美伴其右,
棉球雪袄目星辰。

晨昏三遇猫犬依,
两小无猜倍惊喜。

65 Backache

Backache bothers me,
I could neither sit nor lie,
Swimming is heaven.

背疼

背疼扰我烦，
不能躺也不能坐，
泳池成天堂。

66 Stage Fright

Standing on a stage,
I am going to give a speech.
My brain goes empty.

怯场

站在舞台上,
我的演讲将开始,
头脑变空白。

67 A Portrait of Pomegranate

A splash of orange,

A sweep of crimson,

Some brownish patches on the Xuan paper

Compose a portrait of pomegranate.

A little pink slipped between,

Some seeds look like rubies.

A wave of rose pink,

A bank of treasure.

This just makes out the wish of posterity.

石榴图

橘黄一抹胭脂盖,
宣纸尽染赭石楠。
石榴欲坠沉枝绘,
窥缝垂涎绯色浓。
朱红晶玉籽粒饱,
酡颜潮起玫瑰伏。
珍馐栉比萃精宝,
托福夙愿孙满堂。

68 The Law

The Law and the Word came from the mouth of the prophet.
Whoever listens, accepts and obeys the Word will be blessed;
Whoever ignores the Word will be cursed and condemned.
But who is going to attend to the messages from heaven upset?

The seven deadly sins obsess everyone:
Covetousness, pride, gluttony, sloth, anger, envy and lust.
The evil has more or less in control of one
Who is weak and gives in with no effort.

From where will salvation be sent forth?
The Almighty in the heaven will laugh
At our ignorance and little faith.
He is Alpha and He is Omega.

The Law is written for instruction
Of whose ears hearken with great attention.

律法

天命先知金口扬,
言听计从顺者昌。
嗤之以鼻灾咒降,
恩言感录空落旁。

七宗罪扰众生氓,
贪傲痴情嗔妒纵。
恶性多少盘踞让,
疲弱弃置臣服亡。

救赎谁赐自何来?
至高全知必嗤笑。
世人愚昧少识念,
初始混沌本一人。

赐下律法镣铐脆,
耳聪凡生需听随。

69 Human Selfishness

When we were born as infants,
We enjoyed the feeling of oneness.
As a team and assortment of ants,
No matter how tiny, weak and selfless.

Gradually as we grow we separate and live on our own.
We think of ourselves only with the feeling of otherness,
Hard to get on well with other people their head down.
Everyone's self is living but not human goodness.

People being nice to you are just to fulfill their own ambition.
I am used and disillusioned by their superficial kindness,
When awakened how much disappointment and sadness,
Knowing that the weaker and more innocent endure violation.

Shall we condemn human selfishness and crucify the very self,
And let a selfless "I" live a brand new life like a lovely elf?

人类的自私

落地呱呱啼,
欣然悦体一。
分序宛工蚁,
如芒浮莫依。

日进终独立,
感通八方居。
相遇难相知,
世良几分迟。

寡欢攻心计,
伪善枉我疲。
初醒何落寞,
弱肉穷追击。

唾弃自私欲,
无我涅槃生。

70 Will Love Fade Like a Flower?

Flowers fade after their blossom in due time.
They are so beautiful and cheerful in full blossom.
But when time comes they fade and wither,
I am afraid, "Will love fade like a flower?"

We loved a love that is more than love.
I always think, pray and hope so.
But when life's storm starts to blow,
Who shall company me to walk through the thistle grove?

Your laughs disappear, your brows frown.
We talk less and make do with silence.
Is the first touch of heart and the feel of love gone?
Has it vaporized into unconsciousness?

However hard life is, love shall not disappear nor abate.
The sufferings and trials are only for a while and alleviate.
Love's fruits shall come and appear abundantly,
Harvesting will be filled with fullness and fulfillment eventually.

爱情是否如花凋谢？

花落有时花依旧，
娇艳怒放孤芳求。
白驹踏尘凋落去，
长叩爱唯永恒兮？

爱情以上终未满，
思绪祈愿万虑牵。
风暴骤起宿命降，
谁人与共相携艰？

颦蹙忧容笑寂亡，
片语少言默衍常。
爱潮如斯来去宕，
稍纵即逝落云窗？

生活不易爱未央，
困苦艰难转瞬尝。
硕果爱意将繁盛，
人生盈满终圆章。

71 A Friend in Need Is a Friend Indeed

One afternoon I was in a mood dizzy and dozing,
The telephone rang with a tone ear-piercing.
I picked it up and from the other side came a greeting.
It was a familiar lady's voice, asking if it was Lilian speaking.

I recognized it was a former colleague,
And now she worked in another department.
She sounded so worried and distressed with fatigue,
Asking me if I could lend her some money urgent.

She told me that she was trying to buy a new house
For the purpose of her child's future education.
While phoning a dozen of her bosom friends she got "sorry" as answers,
Trying her luck once more she dialed my number prepared for another frustration.

I asked her, "How much do you want?" She replied 100,000.
I told her, "A friend in need is a friend indeed.
I am willing to help." And I heard she almost burst into tears,
"I was so arrogant and rude to you, but you still treat me as a friend!"

患难见真情

头懵过晌沉,
电铃尖蹿声。
寒暄问冷暖,
熟悉道我安。

昔日旧同僚,
今朝事另标。
燃眉急远虑,
来电求解囊。

欲购置新房,
助女升学堂。
密友皆推避,
试我本渺茫。

十万金缺口,
患难见真情。
倾囊来相助,
痛悔昔日傲。

72 A Panacea to Life's Vicissitudes

Suicide rate rises in modern society,
How pathetic if one loses hope!
Are you going through life with no hope?
Let us retrieve the source of love and possibility.

In childhood have you got parents' company and time
Spent together with pats on the shoulder and disciplines?
They read us stories and sang songs with rhyme;
They taught us how to read and write with pains.

The message conveyed to us is that we are valuable,
The feeling of being a valuable person in their eyes.
This feeling and recognition is a panacea available
To defend life's vicissitudes and unforeseeable changes.

The feeling of being valuable is a cornerstone of our building
That no bombs or storms are going to destroy it with bashing.

遣怀良药

摩登世间多寻短，
了无希望实伤感。
尔置此生无所期？
爱与生机源中唤。

豆蔻束发亲相伴，
朝诫严律夕抚肩。
嬉以传文戏以曲，
读中忍性书中炼。

周遭俱言余有益，
夺目如金众所觅。
得识之感如灵药，
万变不料皆可历。

不凡念比屋之栋，
雷风伯雨弗破攻。

73 On Tenacity

When young, be brave as a young strong lion
To fight against life's adversity.
Success always belongs to those who dare
To challenge life's adversity.

The world is a reflection of your heart
Whether bright or dark.
It shines from within, the light,
A journey, just disembark.

When determined to win
Over your flesh, a weak soul,
You need some spirit within
As a soldier well trained for the battlefield.

To win isn't everything.
It is the only thing that matters in the end.

坚忍不拔

少壮气如狮,
溯流逆境叱。
勇士壮揽举,
囧途往前直。

陌世照心涧,
明暗交辉弦。
耀目明内起,
始发遇征程。

意志笃坚韧,
血肉铸灵魂。
精神金汤固,
将士百战征。

不为胜负欲,
但求终归赢。

74 On Lending Money

We have all had experiences of lending and borrowing money from each other,
But in the present society, loan relationship may become a nightmare.
A colleague called the other day, claiming she needed some money urgent.
I felt shocked because we no longer work in the same department.

She pleaded with great importunity claiming she wanted to buy a flat for her child.
My heart was softened whenever I heard the reason for children's education.
However strongly my mind said "no" to the asking, my heart was softened,
I finally agreed to lend her the 100, 000 yuan, an annual income I saved with caution.

When the debt repayment day was due, I called her but her phone was out of service.
All of a sudden, I realized that she was no longer within touch.
The next day I received a phone call hearing our law school party secretary's voice.
He told me that the debtor was swindled and she was in a distracted mind out of reach.

Not only was my money gone, but also the right to speak out detriment and adversity.
The creditor rights and tongues are authoritatively deprived without knowing the truth.

记借贷

借贷之风普世存,
今受牵缠亦断魂。
一日同事急相问,
久非同属我心震。

为儿购舍再三求,
闻其育儿我心柔。
纵使心纠意仍犹,
十万苦薪不自留。

期至相询无声息,
恍然知其隐踪迹。
翌日闻讯方知悉,
心涣神散其受欺。

财去损困亦难申,
债权言权皆为吞。

75 Peace and Joy

Real peace comes from the Word.
On earth we have troubles.
Neighbors lie to each other always.
Kind people are tortured.

When you hear the Word from the Spirit,
Which drops down like the spring rain upon a thirsty land,
Your heart will be quenched with delight and rejoice.
To exalt the meaning of life is my choice.

On earth peace and good will is rendered toward men,
When you give glory to God in the highest.
When you worship Him in truth and in spirit,
How dare you say, "There is no God" with oblivion?

Men of little faith wake up and revive from your pride.
Humble yourself with a contrite spirit and applaud.

平安喜乐

平静安稳源道生,
世间黎民陷苦闷。
邻舍相欺数相骗,
善人几度磨难逢。

当闻细听悟箴言,
春田久旱沐霖甘。
欢从中来倍快乐,
圣名高举渡彼岸。

和平良善降众生,
荣神赐福唯尊蒙。
心诚明净来敬拜,
疏言莫敢揣圣能。

小信之人得重塑,
忧伤痛悔称赞许。

76 Friends and Foes

Friends love and offer timely help without making a show;
Foes hate and wrong you especially when you are in adversity.
Foes do not write on their forehead that they are your enemy,
So be alert and keep far off the wicked and eschew evil fellows.

When you are so kind to help others,
Make sure that they do not plan to take more advantages,
Because these may not be your true friends but foes
When you stop your free grants and alms.

When I lend a handsome sum of money to a friend,
She spends it quickly without any gratitude.
She serves you with lips' service and shamelessly
Proclaims that she is poor and has no intention to return it timely.

Friends hug you and warm your heart like sunshine,
But foes ruin our happiness in a swiftness from the baseline.

朋友与仇敌

朋友相助雪送炭,
仇敌补刀火浇油。
不可貌相印难辨,
敬远警惕避邪祟。

心善助人而为乐,
得寸进尺亦有者。
解囊资助终止时,
辱骂毁谤时有之。

倾囊相助燃眉急,
顷刻挥霍不感激。
厚颜无耻油嘴滑,
穷困藉口无赖耍。

友人相拥心若灿,
仇敌釜底霎抽薪。

77 Happiness, Success and Health

If you were a billionaire but with no friends, you wouldn't be happy.
If you achieved great success but lost your health, you wouldn't be happy.
Happiness, success and health, these three
Compose life's three basic elements of wealth.

If you want to be joyful and jubilant, please live for others and forget yourself.
If you desire to be successful, please love your neighbors and contribute.
Love and contribution will enlarge your coast and broaden your turf.
The richness and rejoicing of your purpose will be exalted to a heavenly gate.

Only when we realize how tiny, insignificant and petite all men are
Can we achieve real happiness, success, physical and mental health.
We run, jump, exercise and labor hard toward our life purpose afar.
But adversities, troubles and tribulations accompany throughout our growth.

Being healthy and happy is the self-reliant success rooting from our inner heart
Which has nothing to do with business, since happiness comes from the Holy Spirit.

人生三宝

腰缠万贯无知己,不能乐也;
功成名就身患疾,不能乐也。
欢虞安康伟功绩,
富裕之缎三者系。

欲求欢且乐,先忧天下忧;
欲成功与业,先待邻以厚。
仁爱可广心海之岸,奉献能廓胸中大原;
所希之富、所冀之乐,终至圣世大门。

世人皆如天地蜉蝣,恒河一沙,沧海一粟。
知其理方自得其乐,万事如意,身心俱全。
为抵目标坚持运动,汗流浃背,兢兢业业。
不畏前路荆棘满目,狂风骤雨,刀山火海。

畅我心扉健我体魄,成功便于心底固然生根。
日进斗金漠不相关,快乐源于神圣灵魂之深。

78 A Remedy for Self-Restoration

East and west, home is best.
Going home might be the best
Remedy for self-restoration
When you got hurt or affliction.

By going home, we do not mean
Returning to the family farm,
But to somewhere you are fond of,
Some dedication like writing, cooking or exploring life.

In the hinterland of your psyche,
Success and failure catapult you away,
The same distance exactly
From where you rightfully live your way.

Putting your head down and performing with diligence and devotion,
Regardless of others' criticism is the best way of self-restoration.

自愈良方

金屋或银屋,
不如家草屋。
疗伤求治愈,
回家为最佳。

家之为家者,
非屋宇农场。
饮食起居学,
心灵之所归。

心安之腹地,
成败弹袭至。
坦然而处之,
安然而居住。

埋头生勤奋,
气定且神闲。

79 The Road Less Travelled: Devoted to Emily

When we grow up we have to decide what to do for a living.
It's aspiring to be alive but hard to experience life's vicissitudes.
To choose a road less travelled by is challenging and amazing,
If you aspire to be a writer who cares for thoughts not foods.

With some streak of melancholia, eccentricity and nun-like piety,
Emily Dickinson was a renowned reclusive poet whose poems are still alive.
For her to live is so startling and a letter always feels like immortality.
She became a hermit by conscious choice and deliberate decision exclusive.

She had chosen a road less travelled which she intellectualized:
"It might be lonelier without the loneliness" in life.
It is our mind alone hard to find a corporeal companion idealized.
A spectral power in thought that walks alone works in her strife.

The poet lived more spiritually,
And leads me forward enigmatically.

特立独行：献给艾米莉

成人而立谋生计，
降世难得处世艰。
著书冗奇蹊径辟，
口体之奉不足提。

忧僻虔诚艾米莉，
隐居作诗犹骚离。
诗篇书信宇宙间，
戢鳞潜翼淡名利。

特立独行赋知理，
孑然一身孤寂息。
灵魂难觅知音寻，
思絮魅朝乾夕惕。

傲雪凌霜暗香来，
勾魂摄魄向往楷。

80 Self-Reflection

Am I brave?
No, I am as timid
As a mouse
Before each step I glimpse.

Am I open?
No, I am as closed
As a closet,
Fearful of being laughed at.

Am I nice to people?
No, I am as indifferent
As an alien,
Coming from another planet.

Am I diligent?
No, I am as lazy
As a sleeping cat,
Basking in the sunshine, dozy.

Am I loving?
Yes, I love to be loved
As much as everyone
Else who is loving.

吾日三省吾身

勇者乎？
怯懦如鼠，
谨小慎微，
步步警惕。

宽广乎？
藏头藏尾，
闭门造车，
唯恐嗤笑。

仁者乎？
事不关己，
高高挂起，
天外来客。

勤勉乎？
怠惰因循，
懒如睡猫，
三竿日高。

爱人乎？
愿爱之至，
芸芸众生，
天公地道。

81 Love

Is love a feeling?
No, I tell you —
Love is an action.
Love is the will to grow.
Love is the wish to extend yourself for spiritual growth.

Is love an awareness?
No, I tell you—
Love is an overflow of emotion.
Love is the kind of care that is embedded in your heart.
Love is the kind of urge to do something for your beloved.

Love is an action;
Love is the most beautiful language told or untold.
Love is the kind of gesture that shows your respect and concern;
Love is the kind of language that you express your mind and heart.

Love is the most beautiful language in the world;
Love is the most elegant action you take from your heart.

爱

爱非悦情怀,
付诸身体态。
奋发切成材,
精神蓬勃溉。

爱非意中揣,
喷薄流溢彩。
铭心关切问,
无私自献来。

爱非口中白,
无声言语外。
敬重密相待,
心声许自开。

绝世语芳菲,
秀外中蓬莱。

麦子

82 Unfamiliar Characters

With a rich history of five thousand years,
We Chinese people are proud of our legacies.
Characters resemble images and reflect reality;
Every stroke and dot carries stories with profundity.

We are pious people who respect the Way.
Our ancestors started with farming and stored grain.
Pictograph helped sages to distinguish good and evil.
We hope to make our characters known by all.

Idioms rhyme and can be sung like songs.
Esoteric words introduce interesting mysteries.
The sheer forms and stokes induce awe and reverence.
We marvel at their richness and luxuriance.

A popular song recommending divers peculiar characters
Achieved instant fame overnight, an astronomic surprise.

生僻字

华夏文明五千年,
文化遗产荣耀延。
文字象形映现实,
点横撇捺藏深意。

虔诚一族重乎道,
农耕秋收待时节。
恶善形符来贬褒,
普天共识皆仁杰。

诗词朗朗常吟诵,
生僻词藻富趣味。
笔画形态令人崇,
叹其丰富与殊类。

通俗歌谣荐生字,
一夜成字惊思。

83 The Heart

The heart asks for love first,
Being cared about and concerned;
And then escapes from pain,
Especially heart-breaking anguish;

And then, the liberty to enjoy nothing,
And then, if possible, meaning.
Our purposes are unknown,
Unless we search hard;

And then, to take a rest
Upon what we have achieved;
And then, to be an on-looker
And wait for an award;

The heart beats and is alive,
Reminding us of mortal time.

心灵

心灵先爱慕,
知痛着热顾。
逃离远苦楚,
心碎犹肝涂。

心宽意适悠,
逍遥自在游。
上下勤索求,
天命了心中。

功成名遂日,
休养生息时。
神怡心境憩,
奖拔公心益。

生生永向眷,
地久天长青。

84 I Know That I Know Nothing

Aging is an inevitable process,
Yet so dreadful to me
That I become sleepless,
Knowing that my youth flees.

Grey hair is visible now and then
And wrinkles climb up my forehead.
Stepping into my middle age,
I realize that I have almost achieved nothing.

I know that I know nothing.
How dreadful it is to commit to teaching!
Life is mysterious and void.
Mistakes I try to avoid.

Shall I still lead my own way
And let people say?

自知无所知

随风将去难回避,
惴惴不安常惶疑。
青春一去不复返,
寝食难眠愁日还。

青丝白发忽隐现,
皴黄色栀锁眉颜。
人到中年老将至,
一事无成苦赋闲。

自知一生无所知,
教书育人难胜力。
人生虚镜添神秘,
不求有功求无羁。

说好说歹不经心,
我行我素辟蹊径。

85 Nature and Life's Riddle

Some things that flow there be
Stream, time and the current.
Of these no regret.

Some things that stop there be
Loss, anguish and a broken heart.
Nor these befit me.

There are that last and linger
Childhood, memory and the smell of a flower.
How can I expound nature and life's riddle?

自然与生活之谜

流淌的是
小溪、时间与水流,
无怨无悔。

停止的是
失落、痛苦与伤心,
毋烦勿扰。

滞留的是
童年、花香与回忆,
奥秘无解。

86 Change, Energy of Adventure

A new MacBook was purchased to improve efficiency,
But I was a little reluctant to pack all my stuff
And move to a new turf, applying new stuff.
The thought of change is overwhelmingly tough.

Only audacious people love to change,
Change is the energy of adventure.
However, not everyone is endowed with courage,
To explore a new and perhaps rough route in the future.

Sticking to the comfort zone is an undertow in a forward wave,
While change brings more challenges and opportunities.
Romanticists prefer adventurous stories.
Change is the energy of adventure.

Love to change is a symbol of youthful spirit.
Reluctance to change only heads for perishing pit.

探赜索隐而求变

新购电脑欲提效,
旧存打包百般扰。
弃旧换新须动力,
天翻地覆心如挠。

勇者喜新求月异,
穷则思变换新颜。
锐不可当非闲人,
探赜索隐深致远。

安居乐俗回头浪,
乘风破浪创机遇。
不拘绳墨闯天涯,
龙马精神英姿飒。

古道热肠神飞奕,
固步自封命旦夕。

87 Heavenly Father and Mother

One felt so desperate while parental love was lost.
Parents favoritism could least edify a child but destroy.
He or she feels abandoned because of their negligence.

Children are born equal, boy or girl, spiritually.
What makes a child more valuable than another?
Is it his gender or cute appearance?

When parental love is nowhere to be found,
The child is least happy in the world,
Since no one's recognition can replace parents'.

Worthy parents are ubiquitous,
However unworthy ones also fill the earth.
Their children are abused without good reason.

My heart is torn and grieved.
Tears well up in my eyes.
I long for care and love from heavenly father and mother.

天上父母

视如敝屣万念灰,
双亲偏爱豆蔻毁,
置若罔闻弃于人。

男女生来本平等,
厚此薄彼为何故?
玉质金相男儿身?

舔犊情深情不再,
黯然神伤神俱伤,
椿萱赞赏不可替。

父母恩勤芳菲处,
不称职者亦遍途,
拳打脚踢无缘故。

椎心泣血如刀割,
热泪盈眶泣苍额,
天上父母云日拨。

88 My Friends Are My Estate

I never know the institution of unctuous flattery.
Nor can I bend my knees to the influential.
Whenever bullied or wronged,
My friends are always on my side.

The hard-working and honest are not appreciated,
Only those who behave well whenever superiors present.
One small error blots out all the virtues and efforts.
Darkness prevails how can a sunflower survive?

My friends see me and take pity on me.
They are with me and do everything to help me.
Love is greatest and I shall never want.
True estates are not wealth, name or fame.

My friends are my estate and I shall not want.
They are with me and anoint me with worth and faith.

义结金兰

阿谀奉承弗效颦,
达官显贵不屈膝。
凌辱屈枉会有时,
莫逆之交援有灵。

任劳任怨未赏识,
面上寡言少阿奉。
一失足功败垂成,
弊处谁容向阳生?

惺惺相惜唯故人,
清风高谊相携登。
有爱乃大莫缺憾,
财富名誉皆空谈。

肝胆相照真富豪,
义薄云天抹香膏。

89 When We Lose

When we lose the freedom of moving around
Due to a broken ankle, we feel very helpless and bored.
When we cannot receive a parcel or deliver a package
Because of an epidemic we miss all the previous advantage.

Not until we lose shall we get to know the value of happiness.
All of us grow in pains and sufferings.
When we lose some friend because of distance or negligence,
We realize that life without the friend is worthless.

When we lose some money in foolish investments,
We see how hard we have worked and accumulated wealth in prudence.
When we lose some precious things in carelessness,
We regretted that we should have been more careful and meticulous.

When we lose we reflect and understand
One day the loss will be a gain instead.

失落有时

身不由己步难移,
伤筋动骨无所倚。
疫病广传失自由,
寄件收件水汇溪。

快乐不复悔当初,
千辛万苦方征途。
天各一方疏联络,
割袍断义情难续。

胼手胝足汗如雨,
鲁莽投资金散尽。
奇珍异宝无翼飞,
小心使得万年舟。

失落有时常思揣,
千金散尽还复来。

90 Peace Is Paradise

We used to dream lofty and big,
But when the whole nation is plagued
We reflect upon our fatigue
For what is all our toil and trouble doubled?

Why shall we wear our bones to sore?
What disturbs our sleep and dream?
Why shall we bear heavy burdens afore?
What good are we doing for esteem?

Peace is paradise,
Health — hardware.
Titles outside disguise,
Travail void and unaware.

Inward peace and tranquility,
Both are auspicious for longevity.

福泰安康

志存高远冲云霄,
举国受困疫情中。
疲乏困顿省自身,
劳苦愁烦皆成空。

筋疲力尽骨头酸,
废寝忘食为何故?
劳苦重担不堪负,
自重可否添寿数?

福泰安康别无恙,
身强力壮是硬核。
外在虚衔徒虚表,
劳苦虚空浑不晓。

气定神闲静致远,
怡然养性寿无疆。

91 Nostalgic

The White Rabbit sweets,
Memory of my childhood,
Are tenderly sweet.

怀旧

大白兔奶糖,
童年之美好回忆,
甜美尚温柔。

92 The Cheerful Poet Society

The day my feet stepped onto the premise of my university,
I seemed to get into a new world filled with societies:
Roller-skating, the debating team, dancing club and so on,
But I finally chose the least popular "Cheerful Poet Society".

For me, to write a poem used to be a dream.
I think I can live without fame;
However, I cannot live without a dream.
I hate to abandon my aim and conclude with a shame.

A cheerful poet society is a place
Where I may realize my dream,
And I may discover my inner peace.
That makes me feel belonging to a team.

Cheerful poet society will cheer me up, I believe
As long as I keep reading and creating poems to relieve.

欢乐诗社

闲步校园芳草路,
社团百千知何数。
舞袂唇枪踏云轮,
欢乐诗社心归处。

利禄功名儒冠误,
少年怀抱永相逐。
莫作蓬间枝头雀,
壮志鸿鹄挥辞赋。

芝兰芳薰团香馥,
便浇块垒胸中物。
心了无尘静似水,
且共诗友咏不足。

欢乐诗社欢乐多,
文藻诗词如雨沐。

Part III

Meditation 人生思考

1 A Day's Experiment

Experiment to me

Is every day I spend,

If it contains a meaning,

A purpose to strive for ahead.

I admire Jing Wei and Yu Gong.

One wants to fill up the sea;

The other moves the mountains away.

Both think big and act determinedly anyway.

The visible things are dwarfed by the invisible spirit,

However tiny an individual seems confronting Mount Everest.

The power of the heart is greater than imagined.

A poor man's tear values more than a rich man's gold.

Human nature shares love, sympathy and understanding.

I am part of a day's experiment in exploring.

屡试屡验

浮云朝露夜继日，
屡试屡验孜不倦。
鸿鹄之志立于前，
争分夺秒勤为径。

精卫愚公为吾师，
精卫填海造福民。
愚公移山意志坚，
虚怀若谷志高远。

坚忍不拔壮波澜，
沧海一粟攀珠峰。
跛鳖千里不可及，
穷人热泪赛富金。

人之初性本为善，
卧薪尝胆试锋芒。

2 My Clock

My clock keeps esoteric time:
Sometimes a day is longer than a decade
When I am waiting for my beloved;
Sometimes a minute too short for crying.

Tick, tick, tick,
The clock is ticking me old.
I am struggling to stay young.
Age-defying lotions seem stupid.

My clock keeps simple time:
Twenty-four hours a day and sixty minutes an hour.
Sixty seconds a minute makes me rich and affluent.
Why didn't I realize this before?

God is good and fair.
Thou are Alpha and Omega.

晨钟暮鼓

晨钟暮鼓深难测,
翘首以待爱人归。
一日三秋慢吞吞,
白驹过隙无暇泣。

滴答滴答不停转,
春归人老分分秒。
补虚驻颜不停息,
涂脂抹粉皆徒然。

晨钟暮鼓不偏倚,
日月如数转乾坤。
分秒必争富无骄,
过往为何不觉察。

天公地道人人益,
丹青不渝终若一。

3 A Year

The suddenness of the spring,
The exuberance of the summer,
The thrivingness of the autumn,
And the sluggishness of the winter

Form a year,
And a year passed promptly
As swiftly as a sigh,
A regret for the time wasted vainly.

The Spring Festival is arriving,
And I am busy preparing
For a menagerie of delicacies
To celebrate New Year's anniversaries.

The old year passed and a new year comes
In rotation, adding aggradation for good times.

年复一年

春风雨露不及防,
枝繁叶茂盛夏忙。
欣欣向荣叶知秋,
数九寒冬皆萧条。

四节轮转岁序更,
光阴荏苒弹指间。
一声叹息人已老,
日月蹉跎常悔恨。

春节将至迎新年,
饕餮大餐忙准备。
八珍玉食香四溢,
恭贺新禧福临门。

辞旧迎新岁如梭,
寸积铢累祥云多。

4 Friendship in a Storm

Presentiment is that smell of the rain,
Indicating that a shower is at hand,
The notice to the startled friend
That storms are not going to refrain.

You have but one canopy,
The sunshade to share,
But you give it to me,
Because you value me more.

I won't take it from you to spare
From getting wet.
Both of us share the shade,
Wet through but bittersweet.

Adversity is a blessing,
And friendship changes everything.

风雨中的友情

闻到雨味,
预知风雨。
惊了友人,
风雨无情。

一个华盖,
一把雨伞。
你给了我,
视我为宝。

我怎能舍,
你淋雨湿?
两人共伞,
既苦又甜。

逆境化福,
友谊使然。

晓迎秋露一枝新
麦子

5 Reading

I will read everyone like a novel,
Just as a bird tastes a fruit;
Just as a squirrel cracks a nut
To know if it contains a kernel.

A menagerie presents different stories to enjoy.
Reading people and books alike
Takes time and toil
With a heart on a hitchhike.

The discovery might marvel me.
Dejection or felicity is hard to foresee,
Yet reading enriches me.
No matter where is the heavenly apogee.

People, the more I read, I respect.
Books, the more I peruse, I retrospect and prospect.

阅读

阅人如阅书,
堪比鸟尝果。
又如鼠嗑壳,
方知有仁否。

芸芸众生乐,
阅人无数勤。
犹如启征程,
费心又劳力。

未知愁与喜,
所寻惊万分。
博闻识广富,
九天可揽月。

识人逾无数,
谦恭敬乾坤。

6 The Feeblest and the Waywardest

I am the feeblest child of nature:
The first violet or a daffodil,
A bee murmuring in the blossoms,
A bird fluttering in the groves.

The waywardest is like the billow,
Shouting at his mother with a bellow,
The thunder and then the shower,
Rampant like madder.

I am the feeblest child of nature
Who dares not retort her mildest admonition.
I moan and sob alone to confide to the moon my woe.
The waywardest derides at my lamentation.

Feeble as I am I shall not soon perish.
Anon I will rejuvenate and replenish.

羸弱与刚愎

弱不禁风沧海中,
初春水仙紫罗兰。
蜜蜂翁翁花丛转,
鸟儿啁啾枝梢攀。

刚愎自用涛拍岸,
咄咄无拦冲慈萱。
电闪雷鸣盆雨覆,
风魔九伯痴狂癫。

太仓一粟渺小儿,
岂敢驳责造化恩。
形单影只向月吟,
鹜者嗤之以恸哀。

羸弱单薄不甘亡,
置于死地而后生。

7 When Faith Is Lost

When faith is lost,

Being becomes beggary.

Because once lost,

One falls into an abject decennary.

Darkness and death approaching,

Life loses its purpose.

Reform and revival far-reaching,

Redemption can but once replenish a rose.

To lose one's faith is

Worse than to lose one's purse,

Because purses lost can again be purchased,

But faith lost can hardly regain untainted.

By contrast most,

May faith never be lost.

金石不坚

信心丧失时,
生存成乞讨。
金石之坚碎,
颠沛流离始。

暗无天日临,
百无聊赖蹉。
不思进与取,
凋花不复生。

散金家常事,
信念不可丧。
散金尚可补,
浪子难回头。

权衡其轻重,
志矢不能渝。

8 The Simple Days

Emily taught me to venerate the simple days
And to invest existence with a stately air.
How ecstatic and frantic was that day
That I gazed out of my chair.

The dignity and respect comes
From daily life and a simple smile.
A nod of head and a shake of hands
Are all we esteem and file.

What is so special of a pageantry day,
But the designation of a history.
Simple days are just the day
For common people anticipatory.

For the future of eternity,
I patiently await reward and immortality.

寻常的日子

艾米莉曰尊常日,
注以高贵雅情致。
我倚座中凝神思,
心醉神迷若狂痴。

常人相敬且相尊,
在于平日一笑问。
握手点头敬相呈,
尊礼崇意载心寅。

显耀盛日何殊异?
汗牛史册渺一记。
寻常之日简平易,
正为百姓所待期。

他日必能承赏恩,
耐守常日持以恒。

9 A Word

A word becomes alive,
When it is said,
So be careful
With the words said.

Hope, joy, truth,
Love, persevering and faith,
Gentleness, goodness, meekness,
Tenderness, temperance and tolerance,

All these I love
I shall say.
All those I love not
I shall not say.

A word begins to live
The day I say it.

言辞

辞始有灵
于我言之日。
谨聆我言,
慎会我意。

盼望、喜乐、真理,
仁爱、忍耐、信心,
恩慈、良善、温柔,
亲切、节制、宽容。

吾爱之词,
畅言之。
吾厌之词,
谨避之。

辞始有灵,
于我言之日。

10 Deviation

There is a right way ahead of me,
But more often than not, I deviate from the right path.
How can I abandon thee,
The guide and light of my faith?

I would prefer to listen to the weak voice of my heart,
But Satan shouted into my ears,
Do this and do that,
Forget that decent divinity's interference.

Chops and changes come to my decisions,
And I start to waver and wander around;
Life is full of illusions and disillusions,
I go astray in a desolate desert surround.

Providence is mighty and the main might
Only when you fully trust.

离经叛道

吾为人道近咫尺，
三番屡次偏熟离。
怎舍相与辞抛弃，
信仰之光与我师？

愿聆心底微呼唤，
奈何撒旦耳畔谗。
巧语诱人旁侍待，
圣诫抛却空忘然。

万千变化坏我心，
踌躇徘徊畏精进；
幻想化灭盈吾生，
茫茫沙漠终迷行。

天意有情控洪荒，
坚信不疑始交煌。

11   Commitment

Love that changes cannot be called love,
Yet some breakup line goes,
"I have fallen in love with someone else
Hither and thither I do rove."

Is it a must and might to love one soul in one life?
Commitment to romance is in question.
A deep and devotional love is my aspiration,
Yet sacked wives are rife.

With discretion and circumspection
I prayed for a true love.
May he love me and I him wholeheartedly with devotion,
Holy and pure as a dove.

We love with a love for thousands of years,
On end with no fears.

承诺

万变之爱非真爱,
断线绝情说拜拜。
我心已向他人开,
踌躇不安往复来。

一生定许唯一人?
忠贞于情成一问。
海誓山盟我求恳,
弃偶遗妻却行盛。

谨小慎微行四海,
祈求真爱常相思。
以诚相倾同舟济,
心如鸽净圣童孩。

真情相爱千万年,
穷本极源无所惮。

12 Pride

Everyone is proud of something:
Some face and some fame,
Others wealth, health or strength.
Yet I have nothing to be proud of me.

My marriage ran on rocks,
So I felt like a failure.
Unconsciously I started to live as a recluse,
Being laughed at was my greatest fear.

However, one day I realized
Why I should be bothered
By what others thought.
Pride was the biggest enemy naught.

Therefore, I say to me, "Come what may."
My destiny can only be controlled by the Almighty.

傲骨

人人皆有得意心，
或展颜面或显名，
财富体健不自矜，
世间唯我一身贫。

婚姻巨舰骤触礁，
满心挫败意难消。
恍惚身似处孤岛，
唯恐窘态受讥嘲。

一日我终悟
我心恼之故，
流言添心负。
无用是傲骨！

故此自勉"皆可忍"！
全能命我不由人。

13 Family

Family is what everyone desires for,

A haven of warmth, nowhere can compare,

A heaven of love and trust unhoped for,

A caring family no effort spares.

Parents and children live in peace.

Father is the one with wisdom,

And mother with maturity,

Children filled with fraternity.

Parents listen to their children,

And children respect their parents.

All work hard and diligently

With strenuous joint-efforts.

This is my picture of an ideal family.

I cannot wait to build one promptly.

家庭

家和万事兴,
温馨如港湾。
有信又有爱,
鼎力互相助。

高堂子和睦,
家言足睿智。
慈怵温良释,
同气连理枝。

长辈开明治,
晚辈敬重持。
勤勉又努力,
守望且相助。

完美家庭景,
成家立业祈。

14 Grit

Grit is the belief that you will never give up;
Grit is the tenacity when blown by the tempest;
Grit is that you never say I cannot,
But you will try your best.

After years of experiences of hardship and adversity,
I was sometimes advised by the authority
Not to tell that you believe in God,
Otherwise you may lose your job.

When we are rendered freedom of speech
As a teacher standing in front of the teacher's desk,
We need to be discreet and cautious,
Teaching as to present a clear conscience.

I will exchange ideas and reveal truth to my disciple,
The freedom of faith and belief should also be multiple.

坚毅

锲而不舍是坚毅,
银河泄倒肩上扛,
勇往直前不服输,
夙兴夜寐尽全力。

历经万难与艰辛,
不畏权贵不屈膝。
坚持信仰不畏惧,
威武强势不能屈。

言论自由需谨慎,
三寸讲台育人才。
谨于言而慎于行,
传道授业尽本分。

各抒己见存异同,
笃信好学敬如宾。

15 Virtue, Our Walking Staff

Virtue is my walking staff and truth a lantern to path;
Pelting storms cannot extinguish my heart's warmth,
Clean as a white sheet with no taints;
Tidy with everything at its right place.

I walk and wander how to walk more properly.
Life is like a journey of a long way fabulous
To be upright and to others more friendly.
What virtues can make me worthy and righteous?

When I grow old what conclusion shall I draw to my life?
I have enjoyed life while have I left some footprints,
Dependable for others to follow and to step onto as a staff,
Or is it too vulnerable and too void to trust as models or parents?

Virtue is my rod and my walking staff,
At last to whom I should give trust and relief.

美德是我们行路的杖

美德为杖真理光,
风雨难泯心火囊。
白衣圣洁无污渍,
各列其位置整齐。

游走天下安得正,
人生如旅漫纷呈。
光明磊落犹善待,
德行兼备重如山。

皓首苍颜回首盼,
良辰美景未虚观。
后许从迹如杖靠,
坚若磐石父母环。

美德为杖充我杆,
身心依靠安息在。

16 Time and Words

I agree with Emily Dickinson that time never assuages.
Neither is it a remedy for suffering and pains.
An injured heart can hardly be healed
Unless both you and men soothed and comforted.

How vulnerable human heart is made!
Only the maker knows and heals.
But the sharpest weapon is like a dagger
Made not of iron but with words.

Words are like swords that quickens
The mind and the hearer
To respond like another sword or sweet aliens.
I do not mind how people judge me.

Time will bring me to my own judge anon.
Word leads my way and will set me free.

时间与话语

诚如伊言时不宽,
处方无力消患难。
疗愈留痕伤累累,
但除自愿受慰聊。

人何脆弱似蜷蚁,
造物深谙为治愈。
锋利如刃刀如割,
削铁弗如人言已。

话语如矛剑磨砺,
所思所想听者意。
宝剑回锋蜜语生,
他人论断空介怀。

时间最是公正待,
道引指路生自由。

17 Health and Happiness

When he recovered and sang with a jocund voice,
The house appeared as cheerful as a grove in spring.
The air was polluted and contagious flu brought down many weaklings.
He unfortunately became one of the victims of the disease sickening.

The hospital was the last place to visit on a spring day,
Jam-packed with patients coughing and crying for aid.
Jostling among the crowd was far from interest and joy,
When tortured by some viruses of a deadly malady.

Health lost makes one think of ending life.
Death will not be a desirable choice regardless.
Being born, aging, sickness and cease to be yourself,
These are things beyond anticipation and conclusion careless.

When energetic and athletic I shall cherish and feel grateful;
When sick and weak I shall pray and carry on being hopeful.

健康与快乐

身体康复快乐歌唱,
家中如春林般欢快。
空气污染流感传播,
不幸中招病入体内。

春日探病迫不得已,
重症咳嗽病患众多。
摩肩擦踵实属煎熬,
倘若患病更加不幸。

失去健康人易轻生,
离世并非人之所愿。
生老病死人不常在,
无法预知无法断言。

年轻力盛常常感恩,
有病有痛祈祷盼望。

18 The Examination Day

On an examination day the air smells cold and icy,
Both teachers and students feel the tension and worry.
The teachers are busy counting their papers and students,
While the students desperately recollecting their memories.

Why should there be examinations and can they be abolished?
These are the questions often raised by students, teachers and parents alike.
The discussion of an ideal institution for selecting talented people remains unfinished,
And we have not figured out which is best and what people like.

Competition makes life worse and worse,
People more and more greedy.
Learning is not for showing off nor for an advance,
But for knowing the truth and exploring the unknown universe.

The examination day is a torture for both,
Yet we are still living with it back and forth.

考试日

考试日临气冰冷,
师生同感紧张忧。
教师数卷又数人,
学生竭力拾记忆。

众盼考试制度废,
学生老师家长问。
理想机制何时建,
如何是好不得知。

竞争愈演愈激烈,
人性变得很贪婪。
学习不是为炫耀,
乃为求知探宇宙。

考试日折磨师生,
姑且度日往与复。

19 Passiveness

We were born passively,
Without being engaged in this plan.
We will die someday unwillingly,
Without being able to complain.

The meaning of life
Remains a mystery.
Many probe into it as if
To conclude a glory.

To achieve equality and fairness
Is a goal for humanity.
We cannot avoid life's passiveness,
Yet we may do our share in society.

Eat to live, but not live to eat;
From passiveness allow me to act.

被动

被动出生无奈何,
未及参与此计划。
临终离世又被动,
不情不愿也无补。

探索生命之意义,
总觉之神秘莫测。
前人欲问其究竟,
终了得荣归故里。

社会公平且公正,
人类向往之境界。
人生被动免不了,
各司其职尽本分。

食不求饱求生存,
被动出生而自强。

20 Constant Dripping Wears Through a Stone

To save a penny a day,

You become a little richer in a thousand days.

Little strokes fall great oaks;

Constant dripping wears through stones.

I dreamed to be a writer,

A painter, a dancer and a singer.

But in one day I can only

Create a poem, play with my brushes, hum a lyric and move my body.

Everyday seems so ordinary,

But I will not give up voluntarily.

A small step today makes a big jump tomorrow.

The dripping water is still dripping.

The soft and swift dripping creates miraculous holes

In the adamant rocks like bookkeeping and bungee jumping.

水滴石穿

一日一钱,
千日千钱。
绳据木断,
水滴石穿。

我怀揣梦想立志可以成为:
作家画家舞蹈家和音乐家。
可是每个一天里我只可以:
写诗动画笔哼小曲扭身体。

每日看似如此平凡,
但我绝不轻言放弃。
今日一小步明日一大步,
水滴石穿依然坚持不懈。

柔和快速的滴水奇迹滴穿
坚硬磐石,好像记账与蹦极。

21 The Slow Sparrow Needs to Start Early

"Clumsy birds have to start flying early,"
Idioms say and I say I am always a clumsy girl,
Good at nothing like housework and cooking.
My room was always messy, but I feel comfortable and breezy.

When inspired I will sit and write a poem,
Mocking the hypocrisy of the mundane world.
Relationship is cold and distant;
Bosom friend is hard to find.

I am proud of being a teacher of English proficiency,
But some impatient parents good at pulling shoots to help seedlings
    grow
Scoffed me at my detailed and vivid teaching methods.
They wanted me to speak faster than lawyers, just like shooting bullets.

Being slow isn't a bad thing sometimes.
Slow flying allows abundant time for a good view, doesn't it?

笨鸟先飞

笨鸟须先飞。
我自觉不慧,
厨劳皆自愧,
乱室清风微。

有感把诗作,
笑俗世伪裏。
人情冷且漠,
知音人难索。

授人英语我自豪,
拔苗助长父母焦。
细教精授反被嘲,
愿我迅疾如弹炮。

慢条斯理非必恶,
缓步方得美景色。

Part IV

Idioms 成语典故

1 A Golden Millet Dream

Lu Sheng, a Confucian scholar felt he had achieved nothing in life, depressed.
On his way to the capital city to sit for the official test to be a governor,
He took a rest at an inn and came across Lv Weng, a Taoist priest.
Lv marveled at Lu Sheng's low spirit and wanted to help him feel better.

Offering him a magic pillow and revealing a secret:
Upon this porcelain pillow, whatever dream would come true.
Lu Sheng noticed at that time the inn owner started to cook some millet,
And he fell sound asleep, seemingly to escape from harsh reality for a while.

Upon the pillow in his dream Lu Sheng was promoted to the position of minister.
He married an honorable woman and they had five children
Who all became high-ranking officials and lived a decent and luxurious life.
At the age of 80, Lu Sheng breathed his last and died contentedly.

Just at that moment he awoke from his dream and everything was the same:
The millet was still cooking on the fire and he realized life was just like a dream.

黄粱一梦

碌碌无为卢生哀,
进京赶考机缘来。
酒家偶遇吕仙翁,
仙翁援引渡卢生。

勘破红尘赠魔枕,
梦中万事皆胜意。
适逢店家煮黄粱,
卢生熟睡超现实。

梦里卢生官爵显,
迎娶千金子满堂。
子孙皆享荣与禄,
寿尽八十方归西。

美梦醒来事如初,
人生如梦黄粱煮。

2 The Poor Man's Backbone

A devastating famine broke out in the state of Qi
A poor man was wandering from place to place, starving.
A rich man handed out porridge to help the poor man, respectable,
However, the poor man did not accept his porridge bowl.

Hey, alas, come and eat,
The rich man was condescending and the benevolence was faked.
The humiliated poor smelt not the food but the contempt.
How worse he had experienced this life and bended

His legs as well as his head,
But he did not want to surrender to destiny.
He said no to the rich man
I would rather die than be humiliated as a man.

The poor guy died an unknown hero
For his integrity and backbone.

廉者不受嗟来之食

时运不齐遇荒年,
流离失所困元元。
富人发粟赈饥民,
饿汉坚拒朱门筵。

蔑唤饿汉如犬马,
屈尊俯身仁慈假。
菜肴无味空辱臭,
岂因困苦委泥沙。

双腿乏力头晕眩,
倔强不屈认命年。
丈夫宁死天地间,
嗟来安食额前餐。

铮铮傲骨本男儿,
殁身天地一英杰。

3 Seeing Is Believing

In Xi Han Dynasty, the Qiang people invaded the inland
From Emperor Han Wu to Emperor Han Xuan.
The country was threatened by the enemy outland;
To fight a final fight seemed the only solution.

Who could lead the army to win the battle?
General Zhao Chongguo（赵充国）volunteered,
"I am the right man to lead and contribute a little,"
Being over seventy and experienced.

"But what strategy will you apply?"
The emperor himself was much concerned.
"Seeing is believing" was the reply.
The old general was confident he could handle.

Settling down with patience and lenience at the outskirt station,
The weather-beaten general became fishers of men and winner of the confrontation.

百闻不如一见

汉武汉宣战火纷,
西羌重兵当骇人。
外敌入侵扣国门,
唯有决战涤嚣尘。

孰能挂帅清贼魂,
老将充国入殿门。
身虽古稀志尤存,
请缨作战莫隐沦。

奈何胜敌卿可陈,
休要愁杀帝王孙。
眼见为实惊鸿奔,
末将未老剑随身。

仁心德厚坐前阵,
平羌定乱社稷臣。

4 Bamboos in the Mind

Wen Yuke was a man of letters in North Song Dynasty,
Good at painting and calligraphy.
Bamboo was his favorite subject
For its straightness and slenderness.

As he liked bamboo so much,
He planted bamboos all around his house
To observe them day and night
To his delight and paint.

Fine or cloudy,
Rainy or snowy,
Yuke was among the bamboos observing,
Hard as he could as he recollected.

The paintings of bamboo on the paper were as vivid
As the images and poses of bamboos in his mind.
His friend Chao Buzhi (晁补之) wrote poems to praise Yuke,
"Before painting, Yuke already visualizes bamboos."

胸有成竹

北宋墨客文与可，
能书善画学五车。
亭亭净植虚怀谷，
朗朗乾坤竹下客。

竹姿心慕脱俗韵，
绕屋成林作篱栏。
日观夜赏半遮面，
神笔随性竞高歌。

日出日暮几三更，
雨雪风霜不加问。
林中常坐弄墨人，
千姿百态烂熟谙。

竹破纸来墨将彻，
枝节形现心中合。
补之为文赞与可，
成竹在胸实难得。

5 Thrice Calling at Zhuge Liang's Residence

The thatched house was located on Wolong Gang,
Mr. Wolong was a sage and legendary figure.
Liu Bei, defeated in previous battles coup de main,
Was in great need of a brilliant military counselor.

Sima Hui（司马徽）and Xu Shu（徐庶）, both recommended Mr. Wolong,
Reassuring Liu Bei that once Mr. Wolong was obtained
He could win battles and lands of the country along.
Zhuge Kongming was as precious as a jade.

Liu Bei made up his mind to find this talent,
And went to his thatched house to visit.
Twice he was out,
Not until the third time did they meet.

The heavy snow had not hindered,
A master advisor was finally recruited.

三顾茅庐

卧龙山上茅草屋,
卧龙先生奇智突。
仓皇刘备败官渡,
急需军师布谋途。

徽庶二人荐卧龙,
劝君麾下必得孰。
开疆扩土谈笑初,
诸葛孔明一星孤。

三顾草庐借故缺,
刘备求贤心意决。
二顾草庐无所得,
三顾方得蓝田珏。

雪漫寒山无所阻,
终得蜀汉擎天柱。

6 A Swan Feather from a Friend Afar

The King of Huihe (回纥国王), a vassal state of Tang,
Wanted to pay tribute to the great emperor.
So he sent his worthy ambassador, Mian Bogao,
To present a precious swan to show his respect proper.

From southwest to the capital of Tang was a very long distance.
Mian Bogao waded through waters and climbed over mountains,
Weary but happy to show a little kingdom's loyalty
Through their extraordinary gift and spirit.

Beside the Mianyang Lake,
The ambassador opened the cage gate to bathe the swan,
Away it fled as swiftly as possible.
In a hurry, he seized only a feather.

With that only feather, respect was still paid to the emperor:
Would there be a heart more earnest like this than to be neglected?

千里送鹅毛

大唐藩国回纥王,
欲奉贡礼敬唐王。
遂遣贤使缅伯高,
携以皓鹄表尊尚。

西域赴都路迢迢,
山水不饶缅伯高。
苦中生乐表国忠,
卓礼不群志且弘。

沔阳湖水宛玉琼,
使者顿留启鹅笼。
方始浴鹅跃入空,
千金宝鹄落一绒。

千里送鹅毛,至敬携入朝。
此礼轻如毫,甚有诚襟抱?

7 The Lost Steed

Grandsire Sai raised a gallant horse.
One day the horse went lost.
There was nowhere to find it,
And neighbors came to comfort.

Grandsire Sai thought it might not be a woe.
So it was and days passed; his son grew to be a buckaroo.
The steed returned and brought another stallion home.
People came to congratulate Grandsire Sai.

"I do not know whether it is weal or woe," said the Sire.
His son went to train the gallant horse, fell down and broke his leg.
When neighbors mourned, the Grandsire was not so pessimistic.
His son was exempted from recruitment while others' died on the battlefield.

Weal and woe capriciously interchanges;
To lose a horse may save a life. Who knows?

塞翁失马

塞翁有马健如飞,
神秘失踪平添悲。
邻里乡亲来劝慰,
寻无可寻笑掩扉。

塞翁知福自展眉,
门前流水儿长成。
骏马归家偕贤妃,
群友来贺醉中归。

是福是祸翁难寐,
娇儿驯马跌鞍背。
沙场点兵儿幸免,
唯有塞翁少哀颓。

祸福相依汝知未,
灾祸亦能呈祥瑞。

8 A Race Between the Rabbit and the Tortoise

Long legs and a slim figure
Makes the rabbit a fast runner,
While short legs and a heavy shell,
The tortoise a creeping creature much slower.

One day Mr. Rabbit ran across Mr. Tortoise,
Taunting the tardiness within his mind
And saying a hello duplicitous.
Yet Mr. Tortoise initiated a race from behind.

The one who first reached the mountain top won.
And both started with sincerity head-on.
The rabbit, sure of his victory, went to take a nap before going on.
When he awoke, the tortoise was a step away from the mount top.

The conceited rabbit regretted
That he should never look down upon the laggard.

龟兔赛跑

长腿细身,
兔子善跑。
短足重壳,
龟儿慢爬。

兔子路途偶遇乌龟,
心中暗自笑它迟钝。
说声你好言不由衷,
龟在后面提出赛跑。

先到达山顶者为胜,
双方诚然径直前往。
兔儿无忧先去打盹,
醒来龟儿临近终点。

骄傲的兔子后悔当初,
千不该万不该轻慢龟。

9 To Read Upon Snow Light

In Jin Dynasty, Sun Kang loved study,
But he was as poor as a church mouse.
Living in destitution and want of money,
He labored in the day in a farm and rich house.

At night he wanted to study,
But anguished by the absolute dark.
Too reduced to afford the oil lamp,
He waited quietly for the light's mark.

It snowed heavily during the day,
Rendering a white world to the poor child.
The white reflected the moon light
So that he could read and write.

Outside is bright;
The snow reflects the light.

映雪读书

晋代孙康苦嗜书,
家徒四壁破檐屋。
晨起耕犁富人田,
不得余钱添灯读。

漏夜苦读莫虚度,
无灯无火凭谁诉。
到头唯有双眉蹙,
日光何时绕吾庐。

白雪起做回风舞,
万户千门入画图。
晚雪风冷照牖户,
读写莫把儒冠误。

映帘皓雪漫读书,
苍头小仆受其福。

10 An Eagle and a Sparrow

An eagle soars high
Into the sky,
And calls long and sigh
When he sees a sparrow.

The sparrow glides low
And slack,
Not knowing which way to follow
Just wings forth and back.

People jeer at the sparrow
While revere the eagle,
Asserting a sparrow
Never knows the height of an eagle.

Eagle or sparrow
Nature predestines his role.

雄鹰与燕雀

雄鹰翱翔云霄,
蔚蓝的天空中,
鹰唳惊空遏云,
窥见燕雀长叹。

雀鸟低飞滑翔,
懒懒加上散散,
不知何去何从,
不知何事可称愁。

人们嘲笑麻雀,
为何总在鹰后?
人们赞美雄鹰,
燕雀焉知鸿鹄之志?

自然母亲预定命运,
乾坤何人能够左右。

11 Ambulation Is Transportation

Leisure is counted luxury

For those who live in anxiety.

Better be back to ancient ancestors

Who regard ambulation as transportation.

To eat vegetables late in an evening, weary

Is just as satisfactory as taking meat, hurry.

To saunter after the meal to pick some berry

Surpasses taking a limousine dreary.

To live innocent and simple

Is nobler than serving a contaminated court.

To sleep sound and tight

Is richer than a sovereign bright.

Godliness and contentment

Is great gain even for a saint.

安步当车

平日思虑千,
闲适值万钱。
回首羡先人,
安步自当车。

暮倦品蔬鲜,
胜似炙囵囵。
门前车马顿,
莫若掬莓踱。

居庙堂之高,
眷简约之道。
人慕权位滔,
我道高枕妙。

虔心与知足,
圣贤亦求遇。

12 All to One

The rivers run to thee;

The streams flow to thee;

The brooks wind to thee;

The lakes drift to thee.

The ancient sage led his people

Out of the caves to till the land.

They forged the iron and made the tool,

Built the house and tamed the lamb.

Ages passed and people survive

Generation from generation to live

With tides ebb and flow,

Witnessing the vicissitudes and the blow.

All run to one;

One runs to all.

百川归海

百川东到海,
万流俱含载。
风吹水文开,
波浪连天白。

圣君结仁爱,
携民洞中来。
锻铁驯羔羊,
结庐知所在。

星移千万载,
本枝衍百脉。
潮动万花开,
冉冉光阴改。

百川东到海,
波涛复西来。

13 A Dream of Nan Ke

One day a man sat down
Under a big pagoda tree,
Fast asleep and dreamed a dream.
An ambassador came toward him.

He was invited to a kingdom.
The king married his daughter to him,
And sent him to be the governor of a county.
He ruled with wisdom and people lived in harmony.

But war broke out and the king sent him to defend.
He failed in the battle unfortunately and returned home,
Where he found his wife dead,
And his position lost.

The kingdom happened to be the kingdom of ants.
It was only Nan Ke's dream under his pagoda tree.

南柯一梦

槐花树下槐花落,
槐花落向槐花客。
槐花客梦槐安国,
槐安特使请辅佐。

玉庭金凤青紫陌,
乘龙快婿艳绮罗。
仁政施德服乡邑,
安居百姓何其多。

大漠狼烟天子托,
转关败北失魂魄。
返乡萧条朱门锁,
绣帘蛛网垂雀罗。

槐安不过蚂蚁国,
一梦南柯叹蹉跎。

14 To Look at a Leopard Through a Bamboo Tube

Child as he was, Wang Xianzhi was extraordinary.
As Wang Xizhi's youngest son, he was also known for his wit.
When visiting friends, he only made greeting remarks then kept
 quiet.
Father's friends appreciated his talent and maturity.

While watching father's students play games,
He would make comments of good or bad playing.
They heard his comments
And scoffed at him as childish jabbering.

They thought of his remarks as glimmers
At a leopard through a bamboo tube.
Xianzhi retorted, "I am a child and my view might be limited,
But when I grow older surely I will surpass the aged."

When young think young but earnest,
A bamboo tube may be a starting point.

管中窥豹

出众幼童王献之,
才思如父王羲之。
访友礼毕少言辞,
大智若愚得赏识。

旁观父门弟子嬉,
献之一语指利弊。
弟子闻得其评议,
笑其天真言过急。

管中窥豹譬其言,
时见一斑不全面。
幼龄献之识虽浅,
年后才智必自现。

幼时心诚自觉浅,
管中一斑为始点。

15 Grandsire Yu Surmounts the Mountains

A long long time ago, Grandsire Yu lived in the mountains.
Yu might not have been his real name, since it means simplicity of minds.
There were two tremendous high mountains in front of his house,
Mt. Taihang and Mt. Wangwu blocked his way to the market sales.

He and his family had to walk very far to circumvent the mountains.
They lived a very difficult and weary life because of the traffic problems.
One day he realized if he could move the mountains aside,
Life would be easier and much more convenient since.

His family unanimously supported his idea and agreed
To pour the mud into the sea to excavate a new road.
But Zhi Sou, Yu's neighbor came to deride the old man's "stupidity".
"How old do you think you are? Over 90, can you really move away the mountains?"

Grandsire replied with confidence, "Not only me but my sons, and sons of sons will."
God heard Grandsire Yu's faith and sent two giants to remove the mountains away.

愚公移山

古有愚公居重山，
本名非愚以免繁。
屋前两山作云帆，
太行王屋鬻道拦。

须行万里以绕山，
曲折交通艰且难。
一日心生移山念，
繁路化简多得便。

近亲皆允无不许，
拓路山土置海隅。
邻人智叟笑其愚，
山移之时命已去。

愚公未所动："子子孙孙皆有志。"
天帝感其诚，遂遣二神移山石。

16 A Symbol of Dogged Determination

There used to be a mythical bird in the Chinese tradition.
Her name is Jing Wei, just like the cute little girl.
Let the poet retell her marvelous story of that generation.
Nv Wa had a royal birth, as the daughter of Emperor Yan, imperial.

She was smart, brave and energetic,
Fond of swimming in the East China Sea.
One day she met the billows and waves gigantic,
Fighting in vain but swallowed by the beam sea.

Just like the phoenix nirvana, Nv Wa turned into a bird.
Jing Wei, was the chirping voice of the mythical bird.
As if calling her own name to revive to see,
She was determined to fulfill the mission to fill up the sea.

She was busy flying to the sea with newly plucked twigs and pebbles,
Day by day to fill it up on one day miraculous.

精卫填海

柳眼流盼梅尤小,
笳鼓燕城宫中宝。
公主心事谁人表,
身死化作精卫鸟。

惠风和畅戏水娇,
风涌水起避惊涛。
可怜儿童损细腰,
葬身海底魂悄悄。

死后化作精卫鸟,
岁晏花凋心不凋。
啼鸣万里恨难消,
填平东海一英豪。

砾石绿条海生涛,
荡平海波寸心劳。

17 To Learn from Our Companions

In Confucius teachings of yore,
His saying of admonition goes like this:
Among a company of three,
There must be one good enough to be my teacher.

I shall learn from his merits and goodness,
While remove the demerits likewise from my own.
As teaching English is my profession,
I feel more earnest to learn from more worthy professionals.

Students learn from their teachers,
While some teachers are not so deserving this title these days.
As human beings we fall short of God's brilliant glory.
Our own impotence and deficiency shame our glorious name.

Let us discern ourselves and search our thoughts and performance
To correct our own misconduct and set up an upright quintessence.

见贤思齐

古时孔儒辞，
其诚言如是：
三人行与跑，
必定有我师。

自当习美德，
并将弊病割。
授人英语课，
虚心习众科。

弟子从其师，
师难称此职。
人处凡间世，
盛名不副实。

吾等当自省行思，
一改不端立身直。

18 To Make a Sewing Needle Out of an Iron Bar

A boy quitted school and played truant,
Simply because he disliked study.
He went along the riverside to truant
Where he saw an old lady.

She was rubbing an iron bar on a hard stone.
"What are you doing?" the boy asked.
"Making a sewing needle," replied the granny.
"Are you serious, with the bar so thick and heavy?"

The woman told the boy if he could persevere,
Nothing would be too difficult to achieve.
So believed explained why she was rubbing it,
The boy regretted his fleeing from school and returned.

The granny's insistence and indefatigability rendered the child an epiphany.
As thence inspired, he later became renowned as a Chinese poetic genius.

磨杵成针

心厌文房笔墨毡,
男儿辍学误儒冠。
风光看遍心情懒,
缘溪漫游遇老妪。

铁杵修炼磨石顽,
少年心疑上前观。
光阴似箭潜心磨,
铁杵亦能化成针。

乘机警示三两句,
万事可为若心恒。
男儿自悔弃纸笔,
刻苦钻研归塾舍。

铁杵磨针心悟探,
终为墨客不等闲。

19 Old Horses Know the Way Home
—The Value of Experience

A war broke out in the period of Spring and Autumn.

Guan Zhong (管仲) followed Huangong, King of Qi (齐桓公) in the expedition.

They defeated the state of Gu Zhu (孤竹) with a hymn.

Spring, summer and autumn all lapsed away.

Snow covered the vastness

And created new scenery.

Wandering in the wilderness,

The troops were troubled by nature's finery.

Guanzhong, a man of wisdom,

Advised Qi Huangong to believe in the legacy

Of old horse's acumen:

They were animals of adamancy and accuracy.

Preposed old horse galloped with confidence,

Leading all the troops back to their residence.

老马识途

春秋战火几纷争,
管仲随王远征程。
剿灭孤竹计纵横,
地冻天寒难久存。

大雪漫山冻冰魂,
四野茫茫愁煞人。
艰难跋涉凭谁问,
迷踪雪原知浅深。

管仲献计君切闻,
识途老马敏锐真。
坚毅耐劳方向准,
不日定可返紫宸。

任随老马领君臣,
率军奔驰到圣门。

20 To Quench Thirst by Thinking of Plums

A ray of hope, a fantasy of plums,
The imaginary delicacy saved a troop.
When the thirst came,
It tortured men and gallants in a loop.

General Cao Cao pacified his men,
Telling them by the end of the road
A grove of trees was waiting for them
With juicy plums heavily loaded.

The soldiers heard the news hilariously.
The taste of plums was as real as the sound of drums,
Sweet and sour, and served thirsty men incomparably.
All soldiers barreled down the road forgetting their fatigues.

The assumed plums were not there to be picked,
But the mere fancy momentarily quenched their thirst.

望梅止渴

烈日黄沙齿间尘,
焦渴三军怨近疯。
一缕希冀梅子吮,
望梅止渴远征人。

军心大动士气沉,
曹操施计鼓精神。
远方梅林桃李芬,
众军欢欣骑绝尘。

喜闻万亩桃李春,
遥想甜梅也销魂。
军心大振如虎奔,
身疲力乏皆揉碎。

无梅无李杨柳深,
忘却焦渴谢洪恩。

21 The Reunion After Rupture

Xu Deyan married Princess Le Chang in the South and North Dynasty.
"Too good to be true," Deyan was a man of low-profile and honesty.
He held the truth to be self-evident and prominent
That misfortune favored the beauty and perfect.

The loving couple swore to each other
In case of separation, they would endeavor
To rejoin one broken mirror by selling the half
In the market on the Lantern Festival.

So it happened in the war the princess was sent to the Prime Minister's.
She so missed her husband Deyan that one day
News came that someone was selling a broken mirror in the market,
Keeping the promise and holding a strong faith.

The princess delivered her broken half mirror to match.
Husband and wife reunited after the rupture as the before match.

破镜重圆

乐昌公主嫁德言,
德言诚善为人谦。
谁料天理难争辩,
才貌最入凶祸眼。

佳偶别前相言诺,
重逢之念永不落。
各半破镜纹相错,
上元集市尽求索。

公主受俘苦于乱,
昼夜念夫肠已断。
破镜音讯一日传,
忠心守诺不曾叛。

公主携镜与之凑,
夫妻重圆情依旧。

22 Rejuvenation

In Han dynasty, Liu An, the Lord of Huai Nan,
Searched hard for a way to return a young man.
For rejuvenation, he was a big fan.
Every day, he studied hard how to be a child again.

One day, eight old men came to visit.
Liu An was surprised to know it.
The elder claimed to know how to rejuvenate.
Liu An could not be convinced.

The eight old men changed into eight kids in a wink
And disappeared in a moment like a blink.
So they must have been celestial beings.
Liu An sighed, "How I of little faith be!"

The tale of Liu An might be legendary,
But everyone wishes to go back to infancy.

返老还童

汉代刘安淮南王,
苦寻返老还童方。
一心求索为之狂,
日夜研习逆时光。

一日八老上门访,
刘安难掩惊诧相。
老者称其愿能偿,
刘安心疑言其妄。

八老倏忽成八童,
霎时隐没影无踪。
仙人定来自天宫,
刘安慨叹悔于衷。

刘安所遇传古今,
人人皆怀返童心。

23 No Need to Worry

In history once a man was obsessively worrying
Over the falling of the sky one day unexpectedly.
Thus he could hardly enjoy eating or sleeping.
His brows were knitted with profound anxiety achingly.

Some caring friends came to alleviate his pain
By telling him truth about the planet.
The sky was the expanse of firmament.
The earth was the dry land of stone and soil plain.

The sun and the moon were set in the firmament
To give light upon the earth with those shining stars distant.
They were ordained to be there, and would never fall.
What benefits would a mundane worry bring at all?

Thus enlightened the man in the state of Qi was.
Oversensitivity was replaced by optimistic views since.
Don't worry about unnecessary worries.
It will not prolong a moment of life for always.

杞人忧天

杞人忧天忒疯癫,
地陷天塌绝人间。
弥日忧愁把眉蹙,
茶饭不思颇可怜。

诸友皆劝须尽欢,
轻者为气上升天。
浊者为土下为地,
眼界无穷世界宽。

日升月落苍穹远,
星辰撒遍银河间。
万古如斯乾坤永,
忧愁哪如野兴闲。

杞人心如石不转,
空教风和白日暖。
何忧何患无边际,
莫教光阴偷流年。

24 No Intact Eggs Within an Overturned Nest

"When a bird's nest is overturned,
How can the eggs remain intact?" says a Chinese idiom,
Created by Kong Rong's children to persuade
Their father in the period of the Three Kingdoms.

Cao Cao was known to be a man of despotism.
He wanted to wipe out Liu Bei and Sun Quan, his adversaries.
How could he tolerate Kong Rong's contrary opinions?
Bad fortune fell on Kong's family when villains reported him.

Kong's complaints overstated, brought catastrophe
To his whole household, but his children were kids of sanity.
They were neither frightened nor wanted to flee.
They stood at their father's side to face the butchering.

Some children are simply not too young to understand the truth.
They are but too good and too innocent for this world to go on with.

覆巢之下安有完卵

雨骤风狂巢倾覆,
鸟卵岂能安如故。
融子用以劝其父,
莫教人受杀戮苦。

曹操专横骄心固,
欲使孙刘皆白骨。
安听孔融太平词,
满门皆斩树栖乌。

尽日飞絮人薄暮,
断烟碎瓦黯朱户。
屠刀高擎融凝伫,
众子环绕视屠夫。

垂髫乳燕心未熟,
人间残酷性命付。

25 Skyey Mountains and Running Water

In the Spring and Autumn Period, a famous dulcimer player
Named Yu Boya, incorporated nature into his music.
A master player he was, the turbulent waves, the whisper
Of the wind, the twittering of the birds and murmuring of the streams, all his topic.

One Mid-Autumn Festival night, Boya was boating on a river.
Inspired by myriads of thoughts, Boya started playing his dulcimer.
"Bravo," someone acclaimed from the bank nearby.
The appreciative young man was invited to the boat to sit by.

Zhong Ziqi was the woodcutter's name, the appreciator.
Boya inquired whether he could really understand his music and played on.
The melody of the magnificence of the mountains and the streams flowing on and on
All got denoted by Ziqi, which marveled the music master.

Unpredictable vicissitudes happened and Ziqi passed away,
Boya was so saddened that he broke his dulcimer and threw it away.
Never did he play a tune but mourned his bosom friend,
Regretting that an understanding soulmate was too hard to find.

高山流水

春秋伯牙善鼓琴,
造化万千入琴音。
急流微风弦上行,
溪语鸟鸣曲中应。

伯牙中秋夜泛舟,
千思万绪把琴奏。
赞声岸来不绝口,
言者受邀同舟游。

赞者樵夫钟子期,
伯牙问其可知义?
高山流水调相继,
子期皆能明其意。

世事无常子期故,
伯牙破琴心悲楚,
悼其挚友不复鼓,
惋叹知心世再无。

26 Bosom Friend

Guan Zhong and Bao Shuya were bosom friends in history.
Their story was passed on from one generation to the next.
Guan lived in poverty and Bao offered him pecuniary aid, alleviatory.
After business, Bao Shuya would gave Guan the lion's share profit.

On the battle field, when Guan lingered at the end of the troop to attack,
While he led the way to escape, others criticized Guan of being a coward.
On these situations, Bao would stand out to defend his best friend,
Expounding that Guan was just thinking of going home to care for his
    old mother.

Bao succeeded in making Xiaobai the new emperor of Qi,
While Guan once tried to kill Xiaobai to crown Jiu, but invalidated.
When Xiaobai nominated Bao to be the Prime Minister of the state Qi,
Bao strongly recommended Guan, telling the truth that he was the
    worthy candidate.

There had not been two men so deeply understood and loved each
    other
That Guan and Bao set the best example for the Chinese people later.

管鲍之交

管仲叔牙情谊深,
典则垂青示子孙。
得利叔牙多让与,
潦倒管仲杖随身。

征场亏为社稷臣,
弃兵曳甲乱纷纷。
众人不堪多责骂,
叔牙晓仲知感恩。

叔牙辅佐小白尊,
仲欲发箭灭紫宸。
奈何身陷帝王城,
叔牙力举管仲能。

相知相爱净俗尘,
事迹永为万世存。

27 Death Heavier Than Mount Tai

In ancient China castration was the most disgracing punishment.
A man who had been castrated became a great historian.
Being conscientious of his mission he was able to bear the insult.
He took up his father's will to write *Records of the Historian*.

Being wronged and insulted could be the hardest thing to bear,
Yet what Sima Qian did was only defending for a defeated general.
So in his prison cell he drew a circle to serve as a prisoner.
He thought seriously about life and death over all.

In his letter to a friend, he explained
How people died in different ways:
For some, lighter than feather;
For others, heavier than mountains.

So if we are determined to leave a name behind us,
We need to do something worthy and marvelous.

重于泰山

丈夫何堪宫刑辱?
子长声名传千古。
忍辱负重流年度,
传承父业史书著。

冤煞错罚心情苦,
只因辩护战败人。
生死万千皆付诸,
身陷囹吾不堪诉。

尝与友人传尺素,
人生岂能甘碌碌。
或重泰山轻鸿毛,
我辈岂能愁天暮。

若留飞絮在人间,
还请执杖写古今。

28 The Emperor's New Clothes

A swindler presented himself before an emperor,
Promising to make him gorgeous new clothes.
The emperor handsomely rewarded the swindler,
Expecting anxiously for his beautiful new clothes.

The next day, the emperor was given his new clothes.
" Only clever people can see them," said the swindler.
Not seeing any clothes, the emperor pretended he saw,
Striding around for showing off his beautiful clothes to others.

The queen was asked, "Do you like my beautiful new clothes?
Only clever people can see them." "Yes" was her answer.
A man was asked, "Do you like my beautiful new clothes?
Only clever people can see them." "Yes" was his answer.

A boy was asked, "do you like my beautiful new clothes?
Only clever people can see them." "No," he answered honestly.
He pointed out that the emperor had nothing on gorgeous.
Ashamed of his nudity, the emperor rushed home instantaneously.

皇帝的新装

皇帝喜新衣,
骗子欺皇帝。
皇帝重重赏,
焦急等新衣。

皇帝试新衣,
愚者不可见。
皇帝连夸赞,
四处炫新衣。

皇后与大臣,
仆从与妃嫔,
夸口能看见,
装作很聪明。

唯有一孩童,
啥也没看见。
真诚道事实,
皇帝愧难当。

29 Catching and Releasing

Zhuge Liang is a man of great wisdom.
He lived in the reign of the Three Kingdoms,
Assisting Liu Bei to gain political and military power.
Meng Huo, an adversary general was hard to win over.

Meng was caught, but he would not submit.
Failure was hard to accept and admit.
Zhuge Liang set him free and let him go.
It happened about one thousand eight hundred years ago.

Seven times was Meng caught and released successively.
Meng was subjected at last and admired Liang marvelously.
Seven schemes were backfired and frustrated with inferiority.
Meng Huo appreciated Zhuge Liang's capacity and generosity.

Catching and releasing will beat your enemy seldom.
The heart won over illustrates wit and wisdom.

七擒七纵

三国时期战火纷,
诸葛孔明腹经纶。
力辅刘备扭乾坤,
生擒孟获九尺身。

千八百年转星辰,
佳话长存示子孙。
七擒七纵俘孟获,
口服心服谢隆恩。

百计千方皆识破,
金帐座中运筹幄。
得人岂如胜人心,
七释孟获不嫌多。

诛敌斩将少胜果,
服人唯心净烽火。

30 Talent Tested by Composing a Seven-Pace Poem

Emperor Wei during the Three Kingdoms' era had two sons.
Cao Pi was jealous in temperament and Cao Zhi talented for poems.
When Cao Pi, the elder brother was crowned as the new emperor,
He could not tolerate his younger brother any longer.

To create an excuse to murder him with superficial justice,
Cao Pi summoned Cao Zhi to the court for a test of his genius.
Cao Zhi was required to compose a poem about brotherly friendship
Within seven paces, or he would be put to death regardless of kinship.

Cao Zhi was so talented that he utilized a plain metaphor.
"To boil the peas, you first ignite the pods beneath the pot.
Aren't we born of the same root, originally, of the same father?
Why do you so hastily and maliciously plot to heat me so hot?"

The elder brother, emperor as he was, sweated all over.
The seven-pace poem, as a legend, spreads and lasts forever.

七步之才

孟德二子皆英才,
曹植诗才比蓬莱。
兄长加冕乘轩盖,
妒忌曹植欲加害。

冠冕堂皇寻理由,
诏入殿堂试诗才。
七步内咏手足情,
落拓豪英断头台。

煮豆燃豆相残杀,
奈何本是同根生。
同出同源亲手足,
缘何切切取吾命。

汗流浃背欲沾衣,
七步之诗写古今。

31 Complicated and Confusing

In ancient times, Mulan was good at spinning on the loom.
Unfortunately her country was invaded and facing a doom.
The emperor released an urgent decree of military conscription.
Mulan, fearless and conscientious, answered with determination.

She wished to be a man to take her father's place instead
To go to the front to fight the enemies and win glories.
Disguising herself as a young lad would be a brilliant idea in head,
She fought hundreds of battles and achieved many victories.

After retiring from the army, Mulan restored her girlish garment.
Her comrades-in-arms came to see her but were filled with astonishment.
Mulan's story was recorded in Yuefu Ballard about hares vividly, surprising.
A he-hare's feet was galloping and a she-hare's eyes were bewildering.

Can you tell whether it is a male or a female at a distance?
Neither can you tell apart a man from a woman in resistance.

扑朔迷离

烽烟绕三关,
征人如流川。
木兰弃机纾,
代父上玉山。

志勇心毅坚,
常胜铸马鞭。
乔装扮少年,
功名在眼前。

雄兔脚扑朔,
雌兔眼迷离。
乐府传千古,
木兰是女郎。

双兔傍地走,
安能辨雌雄?

32 Three Pages Without Mentioning "Donkey"

A long, long time ago, there was a bookworm.
He loved study but had gained no real wisdom.
However, he always bragged about his knowledge,
And people mockingly called him "doctor" at large.

One day, the so called "doctor" wanted to buy a donkey.
So he invited the seller to his home to settle the deal.
They decided to write a contract for the transaction money.
The scholar thought that was really not a big deal.

He rocked his head and hummed along several sheets.
Three sheets of paper were filled with words quickly,
While the donkey-seller still could not find the word "donkey".
"What the hell are you writing?" he asked hurriedly.

The doctor said, "It seems that you know nothing about prose and
    poem."
Till this day, people are still laughing at this donnish donkey-like
    bookworm.

三纸无驴

书读五车一老生，
徒劳枉然文雅空。
自吹自捧才情雅，
众人皆嬉嘲讽拥。

入市欲购驴一匹，
邀请售者来家中。
合同一封定买卖，
自认挥毫定成功。

摇头晃脑哼几声，
洋洋洒洒数千言。
三纸无驴写从容，
卖驴小贩忧忡忡。

满腹废墨不自知，
流传千古笑谈中。

33 To Mistake the Shadow of Bow as Snake in the Cup

A hospitable man invited his friend to dine.
The guest saw a snake twisting in the wine.
Getting too fearful to relish all the delicacies,
He excused himself to head back to his residence.

The guest suspected that the host meant harm,
Thus he fell seriously ill with hearty alarm.
The host paid his due visit to the piteous friend.
He, however, would not tell the truth to amend.

The host went back home to meditate why.
He sat at the exact place of the guest to try.
While he put the cup in the very same position,
He saw the shadow of the bow in convolution.

The twisting snake in the cup was actually the shadow,
And the shadow of a bow made a man's spirit heavily bow.

杯弓蛇影

众友贤集高朋满，
金樽内有水蛇盘。
客人目睹心惊起，
托词归家病塌间。

心疑主人欲加害，
忧愁慨怆病难痊。
主人探访心悸动，
不肯坦言告实情。

主人纳闷心疑惑，
举杯斟酒客人席。
杯中蛇影赫赫然，
原是墙上弯弓挂。

光影投射显盘蛇，
吓煞客人魂出窍。

34 Mantis, Cicada and Siskin

On trunk of a willow,

Mantis crouches on Cicada,

Not seeing Siskin aft.

螳螂捕蝉黄雀在后

杨柳高枝上,
螳螂蹲伏欲捕蝉,
不觉雀其后。

35 In the Same Boat

When in the same boat even enemies will make joint efforts
To combat difficulties of pelting storms,
To cross the sea to survive,
And to reach a peaceful land to live.

Master Sun's *Art of War* compares
Fighting to a snake.
When attacked
At the head,

It will defend
With its tail;
When tail
Then head.

The army or even all human beings are one in the same boat.
To cross the river is to preserve the ark with everyone's heart.

同舟共济

暴雨倾盆浪涛卷,
横渡大海求生存。
同舟共济与敌睦,
终至大陆辟荒原。

孙子兵法在吾前,
千变万化征战篇。
前军受敌后军击,
其人之道治其人。

声东击西针锋对,
出奇制胜兵八千。
围魏救赵兵法巧,
团结一心为吉兆。

同心同德护方舟,
飓风卷尽水悠悠。

跋

泰戈尔在《飞鸟集·生如夏花》中如此写道：

生命，一次又一次轻薄过
轻狂不知疲倦

我听见回声，来自山谷和心间
以寂寞的镰刀收割空旷的灵魂
不断地重复决绝，又重复幸福
终有绿洲摇曳在沙漠
我相信自己
生来如同璀璨的夏日之花
不凋不败，妖冶如火

承受心跳的负荷和呼吸的累赘
乐此不疲

此生，虽然不相信"自己生来如同璀璨的夏日之花，不凋不败，妖冶如火"，却无数次"承受心跳的负荷和呼吸的累赘，乐此不疲"。

在拙作即将付梓之际，谨以此书感恩一生中无数次奇妙的遇见与思想火花的碰撞。

首先，非常感谢上海外国语大学的博士生导师史志康教授，在我读硕读博期间，鼓励我读诗。史教授开设了"莎士比亚《十四行诗》"这门课程，不是泛泛而读，而是从第一首到第一百五十四首，一首一首地精读。每次一上课，史教授会邀请博士生们起来朗读诗歌，然后开始逐字逐句、旁征博引地讲解，每堂课都是博古通今、精彩纷呈。可能因为我个子小、总喜欢坐第一排的缘故，第一堂课就幸运受邀朗读。我的心怦怦直跳：欲流利朗读莎翁的十四行诗并读出诗的韵味和美感并非易事。好在我事先作了预习，朗朗大声流利地读完了全诗："From fairest creatures we desire increase / That thereby beauty's rose might never die..."读完，导师说：读得不错，以后每节课就请你来朗读吧。承蒙导师的厚爱，交给我这个"重任"。课堂里在座的都是青年才俊，包括很多从其他高校前来旁听的教师和学者，要是我读得结结巴巴，或是没有读出诗意来，恐怕会有辱师门。所以，我一点儿也不敢懈怠，每周都挤出时间去研读十四行诗，反复诵读，直到充分理解和朗读熟练为止。除了十四行诗，史教授对浪漫主义诗歌和很多英美文学文集中的诗歌都有研究和教学。在导师的引领下，我研读了惠特曼、弗罗斯特、肯明斯、狄金森等诸多诗人的经典诗作。没想到那段时间的日积月累无意识地为日后创作诗歌作了预备。

其次，特别感谢上海外国语大学国际教育学院的杨辉教授。他启发和鼓励我写诗，大胆地进行诗歌创作。一次偶然的机会，我们一同乘船游福建大金湖。游船途中，杨教授慷慨地与我分享他描写生活的诗。他热爱生活，更喜欢用英语创作诗歌，令我十分敬佩。我仔细地拜读他写的每一首诗，时不时给他提些用词和押韵方面的小建议，他很高兴，鼓励我说："Everybody can write some rotten poems with almost no effort. 你也一起来写诗吧！""哈哈，好的好的。"他的话一下子把我逗乐了，我心想：好诗难写，但是尝试写几首烂诗，自娱自乐，倒是未尝不可。于是，开始动笔写我自己的烂诗，一拿起笔就想到了莎翁的十四行诗和我最喜爱的女诗人艾米莉•狄金森，我就写十四行的现代诗吧。就这样，从2016年开始，写着写着，就一发不可收拾了。写诗带给我莫大的快乐和满足，一有感动、一有想法，我就写一首，放在手边，心里高兴：今天这一天没有虚度。直到后来倘若不写首诗就觉得生活好像缺了点儿什么。写的时候从未想过要出诗集，只是日积月累地写着，快乐地去记录日常的一些感悟。一边写诗一边学习中国画，两者都成了我的所爱，没想到直至今日汇聚成了这本诗集——《遥有一星似我源——莲芳的诗与画》。

感谢家人、同事和朋友们。在我写诗创作的过程中，你们是我诗歌的忠实读者，金忠实教授、张廷佺教授、张淑琴教授、王弋璇教授、张修竹、吴在华、蓝裕、唐奕……经常鼓励还时不时夸我有才，愧不敢当。你们的支持使我更加充满信心去大胆尝试创作。我所任教的上外法学院的同学们也经常读我的诗，而且还会将英诗译成汉语，加强理解。其中俞悦、马玉臣和季晓锋同学有非常好的中国文学功底，参与了部分诗歌的翻译，对译文给出了许多宝贵建议，在此向你们表示我最诚挚的感谢。感谢"欢乐诗社"的同学们，平日里积极热情地朗读莲芳老师的诗，同时开始积极地去创作你们自己天真烂漫的诗歌，读你们的诗使我的内心充满了喜悦与希望。

我也十分感谢责任编辑曹珍芬老师和美术编辑马晓霞老师。她们工作严谨、一丝不苟，对诗歌的文字和编排给出了很多灵动贴切的修改建议，她们的审美高度着实令我敬佩，没有她们的鼓励与帮助，这本诗集将不会呈现给读者。

由于个人才疏学浅，书中难免有谬误与不足之处，恳请读者们谅解，并给予温柔的批评与指正。春华秋实，笔耕不辍，外师造化，中得心源。愿大家都来读一读诗歌，生活在诗歌如画的人生境界中。

高莲芳

2021年6月28日

图书在版编目(CIP)数据

遥有一星似我源:莲芳的诗与画 = Yonder Star—Lilian's Poems and Paintings/高莲芳著.
—上海:复旦大学出版社,2021.9
ISBN 978-7-309-15781-9

Ⅰ.①遥… Ⅱ.①高… Ⅲ.①英语诗歌-诗集-中国-当代 Ⅳ.①I227

中国版本图书馆 CIP 数据核字(2021)第 117526 号

遥有一星似我源:莲芳的诗与画(Yonder Star—Lilian's Poems and Paintings)
高莲芳　著
责任编辑/曹珍芬

复旦大学出版社有限公司出版发行
上海市国权路 579 号　邮编:200433
网址:fupnet@fudanpress.com　http://www.fudanpress.com
门市零售:86-21-65102580　团体订购:86-21-65104505
出版部电话:86-21-65642845
上海丽佳制版印刷有限公司

开本 890×1240　1/32　印张 12.125　字数 261 千
2021 年 9 月第 1 版第 1 次印刷

ISBN 978-7-309-15781-9/I・1285
定价:68.00 元

如有印装质量问题,请向复旦大学出版社有限公司出版部调换。
版权所有　侵权必究